PRUSSIAN BLUE

Three generations of one family
brought to life

Leona J Thomas

This is a work of fiction. However many names, characters, places, and incidents are factual while others are either the product of the author's imagination or are used fictitiously. Any resemblance of the events and locales to actual ones is entirely intentional. Where the names of historical characters have been used, they appear only as the author imagined them to be. Any resemblance of the imaginary characters to actual persons, living or dead, is entirely coincidental.

Book cover painting by Jim Rae

This book is dedicated to all my Kannenberg family members,
past and present, and to those who are still to come.

AUTHOR'S NOTE

There are stories each generation can tell, but if the next generation isn't listening, they will be lost. Sometimes you realise you are the last link in that chain, and it is up to you to preserve them.

So that is what I have aimed to do.

Handing over a box full of documents, files and folders left in my will to a distant cousin, who may or may not be interested in the family history, is not a guarantee of its perpetuity. Who is going to plod through all the research and notes I have made? So in order to ensure the information has a chance of being passed on and assimilated, I have woven a narrative around the people, places and events that I have discovered. I hope that reading it will inform them of their family history in an easy-to-digest way.

This is, if you will, a work of '*faction*' in that I wanted to use as much as possible of the factual information that I have gleaned from my own research, and also that of others which they have so generously shared, and link it together with fictitious events, characters and conversations to make the whole thing hang together.

Most of the characters are factual, especially those who are ancestors of mine, but also the professors in Berlin, whose names are given in Dr Karl's Vita, and about whom I was able to find some further details online. To give the 'novel' some structure and flow, I have had to either introduce some imaginary characters, who hopefully may have been similar to their contemporaries, or else use the names and backgrounds of discovered characters and try to interpret their relationships and encounters with my ancestors. In a few cases I have taken liberties with ages of peripheral characters as available research is scarce. Descriptions of all the characters are totally as I have imagined them; no photographs have been found of any of the three main ancestral characters. Family stories and third party recollections have helped to put flesh on their bones.

Until time travel becomes a reality, I hope you will enjoy these imaginings and I ask my ancestors to forgive the liberties I have very probably taken with them.

FAMILY TREES

Image 1 - excerpt from the Pommersches Geschlechterbuch - Bd2 showing the entries for Johann and Karl Kannenberg
Image 2 - author's pedigree - 10 generations
Image 3 - Kannenberg family tree - 4 generations pertaining to the book

Kannenberg IV. 341

✠ August Wilhelm Wustro, Stadtinspektor zu Stettin.
3. ✠ Otto Albrecht (Albert) Friedrich, s. Va.
4. ✠ (Johann) Karl-Alexander, s. Vb.

Va. ✠ Otto Albrecht (Albert) Friedrich Kannenberg, * Königsberg in der Neumark 10. 12. 1766, ✠ Berlin 19. 12. 1839, Kammergerichts- und Hofrat a. D. ebd. Dorotheen-Str. 22; ⚭ . . . mit ✠ Susanne Swoboda, * Berlin . . . 1782, ✠ Potsdam (?) . . ., verzog 2. 7. 1841 von Berlin, Wilhelm-Str. 7 nach Potsdam.

Kinder, zu . . . geboren:
. . .
. . .

Vb. ✠ (Johann) Karl-Alexander Kannenberg, * Königsberg in der Neumark 7. 3. 1772, ✠[18]) Ückermünde 29. 7. 1829, 1804–1829 Apotheker (und Gastwirt ?) ebd., 1798 bei Schwanfeldt zu Berlin[19]); ⚭ . . . mit ✠ Charlotte Juliane Schüler, * . . . 1771, ✠ Ückermünde 5. 11. 1846, T. d. ✠ . . . Schüler, Bürgermeister zu Ückermünde.

Sohn, zu Ückermünde geboren:

VIa. ✠ Karl Wilhelm Ludwig (Louis) Kannenberg, * 10. 4. 1809, ✠[20]) ebd. 6. 8. 1849, seit 1838 Kreisphysikus ebd., 1835 Dr., prakt. Arzt und Wundarzt ebd.; ⚭ ebd. 9. 10. 1835 mit ✠ Karoline Auguste Henriette Sorge, * Stettin ? 1. 1. 1816 (1812 ?), ✠ Berlin . . . 1880 T. d. ✠ . . . Sorge, Gendarmerie-Unteroffizier zu Stettin u. s. G. ✠ Friederike . . ., * . . 24. 8. 1799, ✠ Ückermünde 21. 4. 1866

Kinder, zu Ückermünde geboren:

19) vgl. „Archiv" 1928, S. 202.
20) an Lungenschlag.

7 x Great Grandfather	Christian KANNENBERG 1620 (Piepenberg) – Police Constable, Leading Man then Citizen of Stargard 1674-1696	
6 x Great Grandfather	Christian KANNENBERG Shoemaker in Stargard	(1.Katherina WEGENER) 2. Dorothea KRUGER
5 x Great Grandfather	Martin Friederich KANNENBERG 1700 (Stargard) – Gold, Silver and Silk Buttonmaker in Stargard	Katherina Elizabeth FALCKENBERG
4 x Great Grandfather	Johann Friederich KANNENBERG 1726(Stargard) – 1796 (Konigsberg in Neumart - Now Chojna In Poland) 1780-1796 Mayor of Konigsberg in Neumark	Henrietta Maria Louisa PULLBORN
3 x Great Grandfather	Johann Karl-Alexander KANNENBERG 1772 (Konigsberg in Neumart - Now Chojna In Poland) – 1829 (Ueckermunde) Apothecary/ Innkeeper in Ueckermunde From1804-1829	Charlotte Julianne SCHULER 1771 (Ueckermunde) – 1846 (Ueckermunde)
2 x Great Grandfather	Karl Wilhelm Ludwig KANNENBERG 1809 (Ueckermunde) – 1849 (Ueckermunde) District Physician, Surgeon and 'Man Midwife'; Dr and Surgeon from 1835; District Physician from 1838	Karoline Auguste Henriette SORGE 1812/16 (Stettin) – 1880 (Berlin)
Great Grandfather	Karl Robert KANNENBERG 1846 (Ueckermunde) – 1925 Capetown Merchant Seaman; by 1878 - Grocer in Toye; 1890 Dealer in Toye	Ellen Margaret MAGILTON 1850 (Killyleagh) – 1912 (Belfast)
Grandfather	Ernest Ludwig KANNENBERG 1884 (Toye) – 1926 (Whiteabbey) Manager of Tailor's Outfitters	Julia Ann CAMPBELL 1888- 1920 (Belfast)
Father	Leonard Herbert THOMAS 1912 (Portsmouth) – 2000 (Edinburgh) Electrical Engineer	Ellen Dettie Louise KANNENBERG 1915 (Belfast) – 2003 (Edinburgh)
Author	Leona Jane THOMAS	

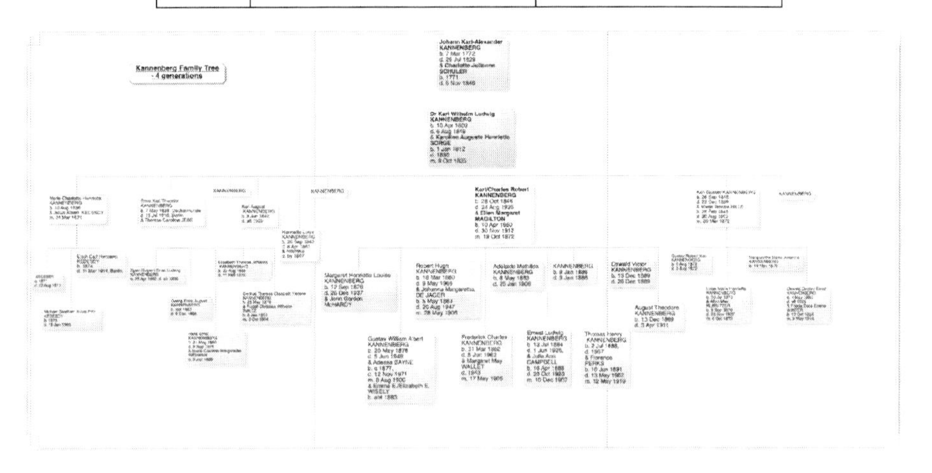

PROLOGUE

Ueckermünde, Pommern, 2000

Although it is August, a chill wind is blowing from the north east making me shiver and I wish the camera crew would hurry up and get ready to take this scene. I already have Andy, the cameraman's fleece around my shoulders to stop me shivering.

"Right, let's try that then. Leona, can you hold the book open at that page again, tilt it a bit more towards the camera so that Andy can zoom in when he pans in over your shoulder? That's it. Great."

Dom, the director, is hoping this shot will complete the day's shoot.

Having reluctantly removed the fleecy jacket, I smooth open the pages in the booklet about Ueckermünde and look at the photo of the river, quayside and beyond.

"Action!"

Looking down at the booklet, then lifting my head to look at the scene as I stand leaning on the rail of the bridge, I can see Andy out of the corner of my eye, zooming in over my shoulder as I gaze up and out into the distance admiring the scene, allowing myself a wistful smile. Letting my gaze linger, I think back over the last few days and what I've learned about my ancestors who had lived here 200 years ago ...

"And – cut!"

The last few days have been a journey of discovery and for those few moments, I recall meeting my three times great-grandfather and then his son and grandson, who would eventually lead me to understand where that part of my family had come from.

From knowing nothing when I answered the advert placed by the film company looking for extraordinary family ancestors to research, I now know my line going back eleven generations, originating in Prussia.

And standing on that bridge, I am acknowledging them in a silent salute of recognition and gratitude.

PART ONE

◆ ◆ ◆

CHAPTER ONE

10 April 1809 Ueckermünde, Pommern

A cold North East wind blew off the Baltic, bringing tears to the eyes of the man leaning on the wooden bridge. Although it was April, the river still had ice around the banks and the ropes tying up the boats in the small harbour were stiff and unmoving. Johann pulled his collar tighter around his ears and clapped his mittened hands together, a muffled sound not even disturbing the few seabirds that stood stoically on mooring posts and bridge supports. It was still early, barely dawn, and the pale light filtered through low grey clouds over the little town of Ueckermünde in the Pommern province of Prussia. Johann was unaware of the movement below him as two figures made their way towards one of the boats moored up at the little quayside to his left. Only when they spoke did his eyes flicker towards them, barely registering their presence, before fixing themselves back unfocussingly on the narrow channel of grey water beneath him.

He should have been feeling excited and yet a huge sense of trepidation filled him to the pit of his, as yet, empty stomach. He had left the house as the first suggestion of light filtered through the shuttered windows. Charlotte was still screaming at ever increasing intervals. He couldn't bear to stay any longer, each yell tearing out his heart and making his brain jangle with anguish. She had been in labour for nearly twenty-four hours. Barbara, the midwife, had done all she could and eventually Dr Barthelt had been summoned and had banished Johann from the bedroom, with a frown and a grunt, as was typical of the man. Charlotte's sister, Sophia, was also with her but it was obvious to Johann from her wide - eyed look that she feared for her sister's life and that of their first, unborn child.

Eventually he had wrapped up in warm clothes and left, quietly closing the wooden front door. Even as his footsteps rang out along the deserted street, where citizens still lay in their beds, unwilling to greet the cold of the day, he could hear her cries, now weaker than before. She was thirty-eight now and although they had been married for ten years, they had not been blessed with children. They had thrown themselves into their businesses with the kind of single mindedness born of a deeply hidden and silent despair. When Charlotte's father had become ill, they moved to Ueckermünde, where old man Schuler was burghermeister and bought, with his help, the inn that stood in the main street – the *Ueckerstrasse*. It was not far from the market Square and on the road to the small harbour, and so proved a popular resting place for travellers, traders and merchants alike. Travellers on their way to Greifswald or Rostock coming from Stettin or even Danzig or Konigsberg. Traders bringing English woollen cloth, amber from further along the Baltic coast or even timber from the Scandinavian forests. This small, once-walled town was self-sufficient in most things and was at a natural convergence of road, river and sea routes.

Johann and Charlotte lived on the premises above the Inn, which suited Charlotte, as it meant she could chivvy the kitchen girls and watch that the stable boys didn't take too many liberties. The inn had been run down when they took it over but, within a year or two, it was known as a comfortable establishment, clean and reasonably priced. Johann concentrated on the bar side of the business, while Charlotte maintained the household arrangements and kept the kitchen running with efficiency and skill. When her father died, they used the little extra money wisely, buying the apothecary shop where Johann worked for Herr Wendt as a qualified apothecary. Herr Wendt was becoming too old and infirm to continue, so the arrangement suited them both. The *Apotheke* was directly opposite the inn and was a large red brick building, typical of the style of the area, with borders above the windows of pierced brick inserts. Above the doorway was fixed a large stone eagle, giving the shop its name – the *Adler Apotheke*. Johann preferred working in the apothecary shop as this was closer to his heart than being an innkeeper. He loved to be there working with the various herbs and remedies, and making up draughts, ointments and potions.

And just when their lives seemed carved out before them, Charlotte discovered that her bouts of nausea and dizziness were not something her husband needed to treat, but were in fact a sign of something she never had dared to dream was possible – she was expecting a child.

A distant shout caught Johann's attention and looking to his left down the *Ueckerstrasse* he could see Hans, the young stable boy, frantically waving his arms and running towards him, unkempt hair flying, shirt tails flapping and the clattering of his boots sounding ever louder. A cold fear gripped at Johann's soul. He seemed frozen to the spot, like the hunched seabirds on this freezing morning. By the time Hans was near enough for his words to be heard, the boy was so winded that nothing made sense.

Eventually Johann grabbed him by his scrawny shoulders and snapped, "Get your breath boy – then tell me what you have to!"

The boy started at his master's unusually gruff voice and this seemed to help him straighten back his shoulders and gulp the freezing air deeply, causing him to hold his chest with the shock of it in his lungs.

Johann searched the boy's face for any clues as to what the message might be, but apart from the drip on the end of the lad's nose and extra rosy cheeks from his sprint, his face registered little of use to decipher.

"Herr Doctor – Herr Doctor ..." he gasped, gaining some sense," ... he says you are to come at once!"

"Why – did he tell you? Speak boy!"

"N-no, just that I was to tell you as quickly as I could, or I'd feel his boot!"

"That sounds like Barthelt!" Johann thought to himself, the man was always brusque. If he could have avoided sending for him, he would, but in the end his concerns for Charlotte were paramount and it was obvious that the midwife was unable to do any more. Now, what news had he for him?

As Johann began to run back up the street, each of his footsteps beat out a silent prayer in his head. *Dear Lord, let her be alive, that's all I ask, please let her still be with me.* He never recalled the journey back home and it was only as he roughly pushed at the front door that he seemed to register his place in the present, and the news awaiting him. It was then that his legs began to fail him. As he tottered into the hallway, pulling away the scarf from around his neck to aid his tortured breathing, he saw Sophia's face appear at the head of the stairs. But before he could decide what emotion she was portraying, Barthelt came out of the main room to his right.

“Touch and go, touch and go,” he barked, pulling at his bushy moustache and struggling into his coat. Johann didn't need to speak; even Barthelt could read the question and his face, the pleading in his eyes.

"You have a son – a bit puny, but he'll live ... and Charlotte is tired, but she's a strong woman and she wasn't going to give in without a fight. I'll send my bill. Good day to you Kannenberg," and with a shrug to pull his collar about his ears, he rammed on his hat and went out of the still open door.

Johann stood rooted to the spot, trying to take in all the Barthelt had said, repeating it in his mind as if hearing it again would make it more intelligible. He could still hear the blood throbbing in his ears and stood pressing the heels of his hands to his temples to ease the pressure. He didn't know how long he might have stood this way if Sophia hadn't put her hand on his arm, having floated down the stairs for all that Johann had noticed.

"Johann, did you hear?"

Her eyes searched his face for some registering of the news he had just received. A blank look seemed all he could give in return.

"Charlotte is well, tired of course, but she'll be fine once she has had some rest ... and you – have – a – son!"

The last four words were said slowly and with rising emotion until, unable to hold it inside her any longer, she gave a little whoop and threw her arms around her bewildered brother-in-law. After a somewhat stilted kind of jig, he was finally released and found his voice at last.

All he could say was, "*Danke Gott*! Thank God!", which

sobered up Sophia enough to respond with, “Amen!"

CHAPTER TWO

It was true, the boy was small, very pale, with a fierce down of hair and the longest eyelashes anyone could ever remember having seen on a newborn baby. He lay in his crib, wrapped up against the cold, while Charlotte slept, deeply. She too seemed pale except for two red spots for cheeks. Her long hair still stuck to her forehead, witness to the hours of sweating and straining she had put in, but her breathing was deep and regular, and – did it seem that a small smile hovered over her lips?

Johann sat by the bedside for what seemed hours, his focus drifting from his beloved wife to his newborn son. It was as if they were frozen in time. His attention only wandered briefly as the sun burst through the grey clouds and began to give a weak but warming glow to the day. Birds fluffed up their feathers and stretched on the rooftops opposite the bedroom window, tucked in the angle of the roof, and Johann allowed himself a small smile of pleasure, relief and pride, before turning back to look it his heir who was shifting a little in his sleep and starting to make small mewling sounds.

This triggered a response in Charlotte and she too stirred. Her eyelids fluttered and as she tried to focus, Johann stretched out to grasp her hand.

"My darling Charlotte, I'm here – we're both here. Thank you, thank you for our beautiful son."

Charlotte managed a weak smile, while trying to lift her head to see the infant, now beginning to find his voice.

"Oh Johann, I'm so happy. It's all I ever wanted to give

you. Now I am content."

A light knock on the door announced Sophia's entrance. Her smile seemed big enough to take in the whole room.

"How are you sister? Your son seems to want to be introduced! May I bring him to you?"

Charlotte's smile was all the answer she needed to gently scoop the infant into her arms and lay him against his mother's breast.

"Here is your son Johann. He is going to be a very fine man indeed."

"What will you call him?" questioned Sophia.

"Karl Wilhelm ..." began Johann.

"... Ludwig," added Charlotte.

"Well, little Karl," said Sophia, stroking the downy head, "your name is certainly bigger than you, at the moment. Welcome nephew – Karl Wilhelm Ludwig Kannenberg."

At that, Karl took a deep breath and gave his loudest cry so far which settled into a series of chirruping sounds that all mothers instinctively know mean their infant is hungry. Sophia tactfully withdrew and left the little family in a state of blissful happiness and contentment. Johann thought his heart would burst, while Charlotte felt that she had fulfilled her reason for being here on this earth and for having the love of a good man. It was all perfect, just perfect.

CHAPTER THREE

It seemed that the day Karl was born was the turning point of the year in more ways than one. The winter, that had been one of the most severe on record, turned into a brilliant spring. Where Johann had stood on the bridge looking at the narrow sluggish channel of water between ice-locked banks, there was now a free-flowing movement of water as the river Uecker made its way towards the Baltic. The townsfolk's spirits rose as mittens were discarded, hats pulled off and as coats were unbuttoned to welcome the sun's rays on their winter-pale skins. Heads were held higher, backs were straightened and lungs were filled with the good fresh air. Instead of hurrying past neighbours, people were happy to stop and chat in the street and catch up on the gossip of the past few weeks.

But the talk of the small town was the birth of the apothecary's son.

"A miracle," said some.

"A blessing," said others, and a few less generous-minded muttered, "We'll wait and see."

It was true – the child was small and seemed delicate, yet April was a good month to be born with the summer to thrive and the autumn to grow fat. No one could deny the glow that surrounded Johann, the lightness of his step and the cheerful greeting as you entered the shop or the inn. Not that Johann was ever less than a genial man – but now, well – he seemed to be positively radiant.

And so it was, that a few Sundays later, Johann sat

proud and erect in the pew of the *Marienkirche*, the little church where he had so often prayed, sang and thought of other things while the *pfarrer* gave his sermon. Beside him sat Charlotte and in her arms, baby Karl, not sleeping but quietly taking in his surroundings with, as yet, unfocussing eyes. When the time came for them to take their place beside the font, Johann felt he would burst, so great was his sense of elation. And in some part, he felt there was a kind of vindication, a sense of proving himself to friends, neighbours, customers and townsfolk alike. Charlotte too, although she might not have admitted it to herself quite so forcefully, felt that she could hold her head a little higher, all the while smiling to herself. She too had found a special sense of fulfilment.

A small disgruntled mew rang around the church as the cool water touched Karl's tiny forehead. Charlotte snuggled him close to comfort him and turning to resume her place on the pew, she thought of how important this little church felt to her, all the times she had said her silent prayers, possibly not even putting into words her deepest desire – to be a mother. As the congregation filed out into the sunshine and dispersed towards the square or nearby streets, Charlotte saw her younger sister, Sophia, hesitate a little and drop back to talk to the Grossen family. And she could not help but notice the smile bestowed on her sister by Franz, their oldest son, already twenty-four and working for his father at their shoemaker's shop tucked in a corner of the Market Square. So, thought Charlotte, my sister has an admirer. Maybe a little encouragement would not go amiss.

By the time the swallows returned to Ueckermünde, swooping in and out of the narrow streets and between the tiled rooftops, Johann had made a vow, a vow that he would do all in his power to keep. He would give Karl every chance, every opportunity he could, to become the best he could be. Only the best for his son. His son would be a man to be looked up to – of this he had no doubt, if it was at all in his power.

As the summer began to grow tired and the days grew shorter, as the swallows abandoned their corners of gables and nooks and crannies between the tiles, a shadow fell over the Kannenberg household. Little Karl was not thriving. He seemed listless and pale. He did not want to feed and even his crying seemed weaker, less insistent. And then he developed a fever. A fever that racked his tiny body for days and with it, deep whooping coughs. There seemed nothing anyone could do. Charlotte sat up day and night with him, alternating bathing his little body with cool damp cloths and rocking him gently in her arms in the hope that he might sleep. Each grating cough caved in his little chest and tore at Charlotte's very soul. She too got little sleep, and dark circles grew beneath her eyes. Johann tried to prepare her for what seemed inevitable, yet he couldn't bring himself to believe it. How could God take from him the very gift He had Himself bestowed those few months before? In desperation he found himself in the silent church at twilight. Kneeling in front of the Baroque pulpit, cream and gold topped by the Lamb of God and a triangle symbolising the Holy Trinity, he asked the question – why?

"Why do You torture us Lord? Why make the innocent suffer so? Tell me what I must do. Am I not a good man, my wife, is she not a good woman? I beg of You, tell me, I beg of you. Dear Lord, I will do anything, anything."

And with that he found himself sobbing uncontrollably. How long he stayed there, he did not know. But when at last, he dragged himself to his feet he felt such a weight pressing on his soul and his feet felt like leaden weights. Closing the door of the Church, he was unaware of the padded echo that gently reverberated around the lower pews and the upper gallery, and the gentle puff of air that caused the candle flames to flutter imperceptibly before flaring full again.

When he got back to the house, he found Charlotte at the door looking for him, tears streaming down her face. He found he could not meet her eyes for fear of breaking down himself. The darkness that now enveloped Ueckermünde, wrapped an even deeper and heavier velvet hold around this family tonight.

They sat in vigil, their hands locked together, their ears tuned to the tiny child's weakening breathing. As the cold light of dawn began to filter through the shuttered windows, they both found that they had lapsed into a half comatose state. Almost simultaneously they gave a start as reality dawned on them and, as one, they moved towards the crib fearing the worst. The child was still, so very still. And yet ... his little chest moved lightly but more easily. He seemed to be resting peacefully and indeed the fever had broken. In unison they broke into smiles and grasped each other – the child would live, their little Karl would live.

CHAPTER FOUR

1811

By the time little Karl was due to celebrate his second birthday, the Schulers and Kannenbergs had another imminent celebration, for Sophia and Franz were to be married. At first the young people had tried to hide their fondness for each other, but soon everyone in the small town could see how they searched each other out after Church or always seemed to meet in the square on market day. Sophia always managed to walk past the Grossen's shop wherever she was bound, and Franz always happened to be by the doorway as she did so. Franz's family were pleased to welcome Herr Kannenberg's sister-in-law into their family – indeed the uniting of two shopkeeper's families could only bring about good.

The wedding took place in the *Marienkirche* which stood almost in the centre of this small town. It had a slender red brick tower which had been completed about 50 years earlier and could be seen from both the seaward and landward approaches to Ueckermünde. That day the bells rang out in honour of the newly-weds and as Johann stood up to follow them down the aisle and into the weak April sunshine, he once more gave thanks to the Lord for the gift of his young son. His eyes strayed to the ornate painted wooden ceiling where chubby cherubs cavorted among white and gold-edged clouds which emanated from a central triangle in which was painted an eye - symbolising the Trinity and the eye of God watchful over his flock.

Once out into the small courtyard, directly in front of the Church entrance, the couple paused and the invited (and uninvited) townsfolk gathered to wish them well. A dove was given to each of them to hold by old Hermann and as he returned to a basket containing another half a dozen or so birds, he released the catch, setting them free to soar over the steeple and begin a circuit of the town rooftops. Simultaneously the couple released their own birds and together they flew off to join the flock, symbolising the couple's journey together through life.

A simple trestle arrangement had also been set up in the courtyard holding a sizeable log and in a shaft of weak sunlight that filtered between the rooftops, the couple were handed at two-handed saw. As Franz squared up to begin pulling the saw towards him, Sophia concentrated on matching his rhythm and making a good job of cutting through the log together. In a few minutes, the log fell apart into two equal parts and the crowd cheered and clapped in appreciation – together the couple would go through life co-operating with each other to reach their common goals.

A selection of townsfolk, and some guests from further afield, were invited to the inn for the ensuing celebratory meal. But Johann was mindful of the simple and less distinguished members of the town, and had arranged for a cask of the ale to be set up within the coaching yard and there young Hans, the very same who had brought him the news of Karl's birth, now a tall and lanky youth, stood ready to pour a draught for anyone who wished it, free of charge.

CHAPTER FIVE

1815

In the little town of Ueckermünde the name of Wilhelm von Humboldt probably meant very little. However, in the bustling city of Berlin to the south, reforms were taking place at his hands which were to influence and change the probable course of Karl's life. One might expect the son of an apothecary and innkeeper to follow in his father's footsteps and eventually run one or other business. But when Humboldt was given responsibility for education in 1809, the course of Karl's life was, to some degree, to be inevitably altered and diverted by Fate's hand.

The town had a school, the *Volksschule*, founded in 1768 but it was run by a succession of retired Prussian NCOs who flogged the hapless pupils while attempting to instil a basic and rudimentary education into their souls. It was quite poorly attended as a rule, the poorer families finding a need to have the help of their offspring at harvest or planting time, should they be of farming stock, or on market days if they were artisans or tradesmen. And inevitably, playing truant while fishing in the river or exploring the reed beds, was a far more tempting option to many of the young citizens.

The building itself, a wood and plaster facade as was typical of the area, was but of a single storey, poorly lit or ventilated, bitterly cold in the Baltic winters and stifling in the brief but golden summers. A lavatory of sorts in the yard served all the pupils and was both noisome and insanitary – most probably cause of infection in itself and often contributing to the absenteeism of some of the roll at one time or another.

Humboldt, though not an educated man – indeed he had never been to school, was a visionary and realised that for Prussia to prosper, the education at both a basic and advanced level must be promoted. He founded the University of Berlin in 1810 and began the reform of the schools system by creating two levels – the preparatory (*Elementarschule*) and the grammar (*Gymnasium*).

It was the former of these actions that would, in time, have an impact on Karl's later life but in his earlier years he was relatively unaffected by the reforms.

Johann quickly realised he had a bright little boy for a son – his only child it seemed, for Charlotte was now unlikely to bear him any further offspring. Little Karl would often tiptoe into the apothecary shop, unseen by Johann, and stand and stare, fascinated by the concoctions, remedies and portions dealt out by his father. Eventually when he was spotted, he would divert any chance of a reprimand with a pertinent and inquiring question, guaranteed to have his father taking pains to explain the answer in its simplest terms. Sometimes he would run errands, delivering medicines to those who could not come in person, or send someone in their stead. Karl had an almost photographic memory and although he could not read as yet, he could recall where things were on the shelves, or in which drawers they were stored, from careful observation. He also displayed an early aptitude for figures and could calculate change required almost as ably as his father.

The *Volksschule* existed to teach basic Latin, elementary mathematics and reading. Rote methods were employed, which gave little scope for the more able or less able pupils. Karl joined the school and took his place on the benches, smoothed by legions of posteriors, clutching his slate while trying to avoid a beating, which usually was for no particular reason other than catching the master's eye. 'Heads down' was a good motto here! Karl soon became bored – and he did what a little boys of every preceding and every subsequent generation have done – he daydreamed.

CHAPTER SIX

about 1819

When thinking of the small rabbit which he had freed from a trap and kept to nurse in his small bedroom, Karl would imagine that he had a knowledge of its sickness, or the anatomy of its organs, if only to be able to further treat the suffering animal. Sometimes he would ask Johann for some salve or medicinal herbs to make a poultice for some unfortunate injured or sick creature and together they would discuss the various merits of those choices available. Johann never begrudged Karl these few medicinal items and in fact, he was quietly proud that the boy took a genuine interest. He hoped, as did most fathers, that his son would follow in his footsteps and take over the running of the shop, but as time went on, he began to notice that the boy had a kind of intuitive understanding of the needs of his patient and that, more often than not, his small patients made reasonable recoveries. Indeed, Johann began to feel an uneasiness – if only in a contradictory way – for he began to wonder if Karl had a gift that would not find fulfilment in the running of either a small town apothecary shop or local inn.

It was on this very subject that he began idly musing when a passing customer arrived at the inn one evening. At dusk, the clomp of hooves could be heard on the beaten earth of the *Ueckerstrasse*, the weather having been unseasonably dry for late March. One of the lads took the reins and a cloaked figure, dusty and weary from the road, dismounted. He was bare-headed and in need of a shave and a wash. Slapping at his clothes with his gloves, which he had just removed, he asked the boy if rooms were to be had. Klaus directed him to the entrance and told him that no doubt there were, and he should speak to Herr Kannenberg when inside.

Soon the stranger was seated at one of the wooden tables near the fire of the cosy inn. He had indeed asked for *der Wirt* and Johann had greeted him in friendly fashion, while ascertaining his needs. He required lodging and an evening meal for one night – but more pressingly, a glass of good wine – perhaps a red Schaffhausen – to wash away the dust of the journey. While Johann attended to the latter, Charlotte set about organising the former, sending the serving girl upstairs to air the bed and going to the kitchen herself to instruct the cook to put together a filling, if plain and wholesome, meal for their newly arrived guest.

He introduced himself as Herr Maximilian de Gräfe, travelling to Berlin from Greifswald, to visit his brother who was a famous surgeon and *akademischer Lehrer* at the new Friederich Wilhelm Institute of Medicine and Surgery. When he discovered that Johann was also the town apothecary, he was even more forthcoming about the purpose of his journey. His nephew, a boy of about eighteen, showed some promise in his studies and he was going to put him forward as a possible student at the Institute and of course, with his uncle being one of the foremost surgical lecturers, well, was it not a foregone conclusion?

Johann could not but agree and silently and imperceptibly a seed of an idea was planted. As the good wine lubricated his throat and the good food warmed and filled his belly, Herr de Gräfe relaxed more and talked less. Soon he was dozing peaceably by the fireside, his head drooping and nodding before being jerked up again as his eyes fluttered open. Tactfully Charlotte approached and asked if the good gentleman would care to be shown to his room.

A flicker of a smile played across his mouth as he stretched out his long booted legs and raised his arms to ease away this stiffness of his extended sit. He agreed that he would, and bid them both, and the other customers, good evening – '*Gutenabend*'.

As the clatter of his boots marked out his route up the stairs and into his room above, Johann took a few moments to muse upon what his guest had said earlier and resolved to talk to Charlotte about his fanciful thoughts.

CHAPTER SEVEN

"That girl!" exclaimed Charlotte, as she sat brushing out her, now greying, hair. "An idle wench ... and too quick to gossip as well! If I have to pull her up again about her shoddy work then – well, she be leaving here faster than her tongue can chatter!"

"Mmm," murmured Johann, lost in his own thoughts and pulling the covers closer to his chin.

"You're not really listening to me Johann."

"Yes, yes I am ... but something I heard this evening made me think."

And so he began to tell Charlotte of what their guest, Herr de Gräfe ,had said of his brother in Berlin and how he was going there to plead for a place for his nephew.

She listened attentively enough, the whiles continuing her preparations for bed, and as she climbed in next to her husband, he concluded his story with a question.

"Our Karl – what if ... just, what if he showed promise academically, and if he wanted to continue his studies, do you think we could perhaps think of letting him study to be a doctor in Berlin?"

"Berlin! But Johann – the shop and the hopes you had for handing over the inn to him as well! And the money – could we afford it! Maybe he wouldn't want to go – or ..."

But Johann cut her short. "I'm only musing – as you say there are a lot of if's and maybe's. Let's see how things go on. After all, he's only young yet."

And there an easy silence fell between them, but Johann knew he had planted the seed of an idea that Charlotte would allow to grow and develop.

They snuggled down together with the comfortable familiarity born of years of growing together. Johann had almost succumbed to sleep when Charlotte murmured, almost to herself...

"I suppose we could ask your brother Otto about it ..."

And so they both slipped into repose, their subconscious thoughts making up dreams and imaginings about what might be.

CHAPTER EIGHT

1820

Although a simple man, Johann could sense in young Karl the spark of innate intelligence that could be kindled and fanned to lead to greater things. And as he had vowed to Holy God all those years before – his son would have the best of chances he could give him. Johann could not help but compare him with the other village children – and to be honest, there was no comparison.

Sophia, Charlotte's sister, had been producing offspring on a regular basis since her marriage to Franz eight years ago. Thanks be to God, they now had three healthy children. The oldest boy, Friedrich, was a rascal of seven and already getting a reputation as a practical joker. Only last week he had crept up to old Victor, who was dozing in the weak April sun on a bench near the market square and tied his boot laces together. Hiding behind a bench he then gave a loud shrill blast on the grass stalk held between his thumbs and the inevitable happened.

Luckily Victor sustained no injuries, but it was Johann who spied what had happened from his shop window and caught up with young Friedrich as he dived down the alleyway behind the apothecary shop. For his mischief he got a severe talking-to, and good cuff round the ear, and was marched in disgrace across the square to his father's shop, where he received another cuff – this time from Franz. Johann left Franz to deal with the rest of the boy's punishment, but as he left and looked over his shoulder he was sure he could spot a mischievous smirk on Friedrich's face as he turned to scowl at his uncle Johann.

'Well, at least my Karl would not get up to such nonsense ....' he thought to himself, but then he began to smile as he remembered the tricks he had played on his own grandfather – Martin, who had been a gold, silver and silk buttonmaker in Stargard. Although Johann had grown up in Konigsberg in Neumark, his father had taken his two older sisters, Johanna and Dorothea, and his older brother Otto to see their old grandfather one summer as he was then very old and unable to make the journey to visit the family at their home, seventy kilometres away. Indeed, he had died by the time Johann was seven years old, but there had still been time to play tricks! Poor old Grandfather was deaf and almost blind, years of close handiwork by inefficient candlelight taking its toll on his eyes. Johann never knew his grandmother, Katharina, as she had died the year he had been born.

Smiling ruefully, he remembered the clout his father had given him when he discovered he had blocked up the stems of every one of grandfather's pipes. Even now, he could feel the shame that followed the deed. Yes – well, maybe boys would be boys!

But Karl – Karl was the bookish one, already becoming skilled in all his subjects. He could read the Bible fluently and indeed, Charlotte often asked him to do so aloud to her as she admitted that she had never been a great scholar and, anyway, she could concentrate better if she heard the 'good word' out loud. Karl's written hand was both legible and neatly formed and his skill in arithmetic was boundless – in fact, he could tally and total quicker (and more accurately) than his schoolmaster – to the sniggers of his classmates and the fury of the teacher. Indeed, the school suffered from having irregular staff – usually the Church verger would run it for a while until another master could be hired, but as wages were poor and conditions inadequate, it was not really surprising that the bright pupils were not stretched, or the poor ones helped or encouraged. Absenteeism was rife and little effort was made by some parents to encourage attendance, especially if extra hands were needed in the shops or fields nearby.

But Karl – he attended without a moan and had never missed a day, except for when he had chicken pox two years previously. But student was surpassing master, and the latest schoolteacher, Herr Volk – a young student theologian, was at pains to say as much to Johann when he came to the inn in the evenings to thaw out his bones by the roaring fire and to carefully count out his *groschen* for a simple meal to fill his grumbling belly. His time in the village school was merely a stop gap and a way to maintain himself until a Church living, which was his ambition, would turn up and he could take up the post of '*pfarrer*'.

However, he was schooled in Latin and Greek and to try to keep Karl busy (and from watching over his teacher's errors) he began to set him more challenging texts in the two languages. To some extent this backfired, however, as Karl enjoyed the challenge and showed such aptitude that he completed the work quickly and demanded more. Children left the *Elementarschule* at the age of thirteen or so, and Karl had just turned eleven, so Johann felt it was time to consider the future.

The door flew open one stormy April evening and Herr Volk entered the inn, the raindrops standing proud on his rough woollen cloak, his fair hair plastered flat and rivulets dripping down his cheeks and forehead.

"Come in, come in!" exhorted Johann, taking the young man's cape and shaking it, causing a shower of droplets to sizzle and spit as they flew into the fireplace.

"Thank you Johann – a glass of beer if you please, an –

does your good wife recommend the soup?"

"Of course, Herr Volk – I will instruct Cook to heat you up some thick vegetable broth," said Charlotte, who always became a bit maternal with the fair young man. "Sit yourself by the fire and we'll soon have you warmed up," and with that she bustled off behind the counter to the kitchens beyond.

A while later Volk was warmer, drier, and his hunger in some measure assuaged. Charlotte had added a few chunks of her rough brown bread to the repast offered (and, as usual, she made no charge). Volk dug in his pockets and pulled out the few coins, counting out those needed to pay for the evening's repast, and then counting out and sorting the remainder to gauge if he could afford another beer. He had – just, and while he pocketed the remainder, he indicated to Johann that another beer would be welcome.

It was not busy in the inn, and the one or two regulars were at present well-served, so Johann took the opportunity to join the young man at the high-backed bench by the fire.

"Herr Volk – may I speak to you about my son Karl for a few moments?"

"Of course, Johann. You know, he is a very able student – would that a few more were," he added with a wry smile.

"Thank you for saying that – "

" – Oh, I'm not being polite," interrupted the teacher, "I'm being totally honest with you. That boy has a remarkable ability to learn – in fact, I cannot do him justice. Now, if he lived in Berlin or one of the other's big cities, just think of the education he might have. There he really would be challenged and encouraged properly."

And then realising that perhaps Johann would take this as a slight against the small town of Ueckermünde, he added hastily, "Not that you don't do your best for him, Johann. But I feel he could achieve so much more than a basic elementary education can provide."

"In that, Herr Volk, we are indeed in perfect agreement. In fact, I have been thinking about this for some time. I want more for my son than to be an innkeeper or shop-keeper in Ueckermünde – not that there's anything wrong with that. I know that he can do better for himself than that, and I don't want to see him growing up frustrated and resentful because he wasn't able to follow his heart, owing to a sense of duty to me."

"You are very astute, Johann. But what do you think the boy might want to do?"

"I've watched him over the years – since he was a little boy he has taken an interest in the medicines in the *Apotheke*. He always asked what they were for and how to administer them. And then he began treating whatever he could find – sick or injured rabbits, cats, birds ... And some of them did recover. Lately, those that didn't survive he has cut open. Not out of gruesome curiosity, but with a yearning to discover what went wrong and to find out more about the science of life. I think he could be a doctor. He has a genuine care for living things. He listens to what the customers tell me in the shop and often before I can prescribe a remedy, he has made a suggestion, or even questioned the poor souls with most searching enquiries. They can be quite taken aback, let me tell you!"

"Well – if what you say is right, Johann, you should think about sending him to continue his schooling somewhere that will give him skills in Latin and Greek, as well as the other subjects required for entry into the medical training Institute in Berlin. There is really nowhere near here that can do that for him – unless you consider a private tutor?"

"I see – well, we have saved a bit of money, and I cannot deny that both businesses are doing well. I suppose it's the only advantage to having but one child – you can invest it all on them."

Across the room, a customer waved a request for more drink and so Johann took his leave of Volk and returned to his familiar position behind the bar, all the while mulling over what Volk had said.

CHAPTER NINE

1820

My dear brother Otto ,

You know I am not much of a correspondent, but I must put pen to paper to request of you some information.

Your nephew Karl is doing very well at his studies – indeed the teacher he has at present (a theologian who is looking to be a pfarrer in time) is full of praise for his academic abilities. He is excelling at learning Latin and Greek in addition to his other lessons and has an aptitude for these.

In your successful position in Berlin I know you must have contact with many people from different levels of society. What I am desirous of discovering is whether there is a good school in or near Berlin where Karl might go to extend his learning with a view to him applying for a place at the Institute to train to be a doctor. I am sadly lacking in knowledge of such things and would ask you to do this on my behalf.

Charlotte and I send our warmest good wishes to your good wife Ernestina, your children, and of course, yourself.

God preserve you in good health.
Your brother,
Johann

As he completed reading his letter aloud to Charlotte, he sat back from the table and looked enquiringly at her for comment.

"That is good Johann. But do you think Otto will do this for you? After all, he must be very busy and much in demand for his wisdom."

Charlotte was always a little in awe of Johann's older brother Otto, who had risen to the lofty heights of Supreme Court judge in Berlin. He was six years older than Johann and she had only met him once when they had made a trip to Berlin in 1797, some thirteen years earlier to join in the celebrations for the accession of Friedrich Wilhelm III to the throne. They had taken days to travel along the bumpy rutted roads of Pomerania and south into the province of Brandenburg. As they entered Berlin, and made their way by smaller carriage to the *Wilhelmstrasse*, Charlotte became more and more nervous of meetings Otto and his wife Ernestina.

Their home was grand (by Charlotte's standards) and she was not a little overawed by the furnishings and the number of rooms at their disposal. Although her father might have been Herr Schuler, Mayor of the Ueckermünde, the Berlin Kannenbergs were certainly of much higher standing. However, Charlotte was quick to remind herself that Johann and Otto's father had been Mayor of Konigsberg and so they had all come from almost equal beginnings.

Ernestina had loved to fuss over them both and show them this portrait of her dear Otto and that silver-covered glass decanter presented to her dear Otto. After a while Charlotte had begun to tire of her constant 'showing off' and it took some effort to bite her tongue on occasions. Nevertheless, the couple had made them very welcome and they were taken to some of the best places in Berlin.

To stroll through the *Tiergarten* or down the *Unter der Linden* on Johann's arm was wonderful. They had stopped by the equestrian statue to Friedrich the Great, the new king's grandfather, and further on had stood to admire the facade of the Opera House. In the distance was the *Schloss*, an imposing rectangular building, four storeys high with a balustrade all around the roof. The two imposing doorways stood equidistant from the centre and their columned supports reached the full height of the building. There seemed to be a thousand windows, all sparkling in the sunshine. As they stood, the state coach had come into view and inside sat the new King and his wife Louise. How fine they had looked, how her jewels sparkled – but all too soon, the coach had pulled into the courtyard and out of sight of the cheering crowds. Around them bustled the people of Berlin, rich and poor alike, but all happy to stroll along and take the air on this beautiful day, on this auspicious day of a new reign.

Another trip they had taken was to visit Potsdam, about thirty kilometres from Berlin, an altogether quainter place on a more manageable scale. They had explored the small streets and stood looking into the water from the small bridges that spanned the canals. They had time to visit the *Nikolaikirche* and admire its cool calm interior. Sometimes one or two of Otto's younger children had accompanied them and Charlotte had daydreamed of the day when she might have children.

All too soon it was time for them to return and Charlotte dreaded the rough roads that would take them the 170 kilometres or so back to Ueckermünde. Ernestina had clucked around them as they took their leave, although by now Charlotte had begun to see deeper into the character of her sister-in-law and to realise that she was the perfect foil for her quiet, maybe even stolid, husband. She took entertaining the great and the good in her stride and ran the house efficiently, keeping the servants in good order. She was both thrifty and generous in good measure, and their children were growing up with a healthy respect for what they had, as well as the needs of others less fortunate than themselves. Indeed, it looked as though Charlotte's eldest nephew Alexander, had a feeling for law and might study in Berlin, in the hope of following his father's profession.

Charlotte had realised that Ernestina was not really showing off in that sense, but was simply so proud of her husband that she wished to share it with her in-laws. As they got to know each other better, Charlotte would tell her about Johann and her pride would show as well as she told of his two businesses and how well respected he was in their little town. Ernestina applauded their hard work and was pleased to find she had an equally level-headed and common-sense sister-in-law. Together they had shared their hopes for the future – Ernestina's aspirations for her children and their future, while Charlotte merely hoped that she, too, could one day experience motherhood. She had even divulged her silent prayer made at the *Nikolaikirche* on their trip to Potsdam – her prayer for a child.

And as they had taken their leave, Ernestina and Charlotte embraced with shared and equal affection. Johann exhorted his brother to travel north to visit with them if ever he could be persuaded to take time away from his job, but inwardly they all knew this was more in the form of a polite request rather than a likely possibility. And to be honest, Charlotte felt their humble home could in no way compete with the relative splendour and hospitality which had been shown to them in Berlin.

CHAPTER TEN

1820

My dear younger brother Johann,
I am in receipt of your letter and have indeed done as you urged me and from enquiring among those with such knowledge, I have endeavoured to secure you the information of which you were desirous.

There are a number of good schools in Berlin where young men may study and refine the knowledge of the Classics but from my further inquiries I spoke to one gentleman, Herr Bernard Wenzel who has just taken over the running of the Gymnasium at Seddin about 50 kilometres from Berlin and some 15 kilometres from Potsdam. He has been expressly appointed as the Direktor of the school in order to upgrade it to one of the new 'Gelehrtenschulen' intended for boys proceeding to the universities. He informs me that should your son Karl be able to fulfil the entrance requirements, he would be pleased to consider assigning him a place when he has attained the age of 13 years (the minimum).

If you wish, I will approach Herr Wenzel again on your behalf and make any arrangements required. Otherwise, inform me of your thoughts and I will act as you instruct – you may contact Herr Wenzel personally if you wish, or indeed you may prefer to reconsider your options.

My good wife sends her hopes for your and Charlotte's continued good health.

Your brother, Otto

The letter arrived with the other mail on the coach run

by the *Thorn und Taxis* organisation. It called at Ueckermünde bringing travellers en-route to Greifswald or Stralsund in one direction, and to Berlin, Stettin or Danzig in the other. The *'fahrende post'* usually had little mail for the citizens of Ueckermünde; one or two items for the Burghermeister and town council perhaps and, today, one for Herr Kannenberg, postmarked Berlin.

He painstakingly read it aloud to Charlotte who sat in silence, as was her way when mulling over her thoughts. After some time her only words were, "Well, you'll have to have a talk with Karl now."

Later that evening, when the inn was closed and Johann had bid goodnight to the last few customers who needed reminding that their beds (and no doubt their wives) were waiting, he climbed the stairs to Karl's room.

Although it was late Karl was not asleep – indeed he was reading from a Latin book that Herr Volk had lent him, and such was his concentration that for a moment he didn't notice Johann standing beyond the glow of the single candle by his bedside. When he did become aware of his father's presence, he looked up and smiled in apology.

"I'm sorry I'm not asleep yet father – it's just that I'd became so interested in reading about Julius Caesar at the Rubicon that ..."

Johann interrupted his son's apology with a wave of his hand as if pushing it aside. "No matter – I saw the light of the candle and would have snuffed it had you fall into slumber. Karl – did you notice that there was a letter for me today?"

"Yes I did. Was it bad news father? You have been very quiet all day."

"No my son, not bad news, but news which will cause us

all to have to make some decisions regarding the future – your future, to be more exact."

At this Karl looked both surprised and a little apprehensive. Seeing his concern Johann reassured him by laying his hand on his shoulder and seating himself on the edge of the simple wooden bed over which a woollen blanket had been thrown, atop a homespun linen sheet, to keep away the chills of the late May evening. He hesitated, uncertain of how to broach the subject and anxious to put his son at his ease.

"Karl, you enjoy your schooling, do you not?"

"Yes, yes, I'd do – but already I can read all the German readers that are there and Herr Volk says he will have to find something else for me to read in Greek, if I am to improve in that. I do little work now as I am usually asked to help the slower pupils. That's all right, isn't it father?"

"Of course Karl – but you must have thought about the future and what more learning you could undertake?"

"I suppose so – I just assumed I would go to the *Gymnasium* at Pasewalk like the other boys."

"And then what?

"Well – I suppose after that I'll work to get my registration as an apothecary and then be able to help you in the *Apotheke*. And of course, there's the inn."

"Did you ever think ... do you ever dream of what you would really like to do – if you could?

At this Karl looked pensive and seemed to search deeper into his soul. A moment later a brightness came into his eyes, and he took a deep breath as he met his father's gaze.

"I ... I would really love to continue my studies – I'd love to learn more and become proficient in both Latin and Greek. If there was a chance I could study at the new Humboldt University in Berlin that Herr Volk told me of – well that would be wonderful!"

"And if you could study – what would you like to be after that?" Johann held his breath waiting to see what was in his son's heart – minister, lawyer, or ...

Without delay Karl replied, "I want to be a doctor, father. I want to heal the sick and combat disease and ease the suffering of those that medicine cannot help at present. I want to ..."

Johann's laughter cut Karl short.

In answer to his quizzical look, Johann explained, "Slow down! One thing at a time young man! You cannot change the world overnight you know! But, what you have just said makes me – us, your mother and I, very happy. We could see that you were a good scholar and we want only the best for you. But I wanted the choice to be yours, however our thoughts seem to be in perfect accord. I would be so proud if my son became a doctor."

And with that he leant forward and clasped the boy to his chest, squeezing him so firmly that he could feel the boy's heartbeat through his thin nightclothes. Sitting back and releasing his grasp, he then told the boy of his conversation with Herr de Gräfe and with Herr Volk, and how he had written to his brother Otto in Berlin with a request, the reply to which had arrived that very day.

But there was one problem – and one that both Charlotte and he had discussed earlier that evening. How would Karl feel about leaving his home to go to a school so far away? He knew how he was feeling, but he didn't want to let the boy see the wrench he already felt. Karl now began to comprehend the whole picture and bent his head a little as he considered his feelings.

"Father, more than anything else I want to study hard and make you and mother proud of me. I love you both and the thought of leaving you causes me to feel a little frightened. But, I know I can work hard and I think that I will just have to get used to the idea. I would like to do this. Father, please tell me more about the school at Seddin."

"Well, that's what we have to find out. I will write a letter to Herr Direktor and find out answers to all our questions. It has to be what you want too, Karl. Now, try to get some sleep. Sweet dreams – and we'll talk more in the morning."

With that he took his leave of his son, snuffing the candle as he left, leaving Karl to lie back in the darkness, his mind whirling with all that he had heard. Sweet dreams! How could he possibly sleep with all these thoughts dancing around his head!

CHAPTER ELEVEN

In due course a letter arrived from Seddin wherein the *Direktor* of the *Gymnasium* was pleased to offer a place to the apothecary's young son. Indeed, if the letter which had accompanied the application from the *Pfarrer* and local schoolmaster could be believed, Karl would be an asset to the school and worthy of encouragement.

A variety of emotions were to be seen around the wooden table which filled the dimly lit kitchen and around which they sat, each with their own thoughts and painfully aware that none of them wished to be the first to break the silence. In the end it was Charlotte who did so – but with the merest intake of breath and shrug of her shoulders. Karl and Johann exchanged glances, each trying to read the other's thoughts. Was there a gleam in Johann's eyes – or was it the merest hint of a tear? Busying herself with lighting some candles to illuminate the cosy room, Charlotte kept her back to her family and her thoughts to herself. But in the end it was she who sealed the agreement.

"You will need some new clothes – you are growing at such a rate. We do not want you to look like a peasant's son!"

As if a tap had been turned on, everyone seemed to be talking at once. Where would he board? Who would take him there? What books would he need? Would he be able to return for holidays? How long did it take to get there? Could he take his pet mouse?

And so, in this manner, it seemed all was settled.

Indeed, the practicalities of the situation were the first

things which needing sorting out. From further enquiries it appeared that there were a few rooms available which the school authorities made available to boarders. So that was one problem sorted. The local mail coaches which ran from Ueckermünde to Berlin would take Karl the 170 kilometres there and then, on arrival in Berlin, Uncle Otto would collect him. The following day he would be put on the local coach to Potsdam, and it was arranged that he would be collected from the coaching stop there by a representative of the school and then taken to Seddin.

And so it was, as the days of summer were shortening and just the hint of autumn was in the air, that Karl stood outside the Inn where he had watched so many travellers and coaches come and go through his childhood years, but this time he was the one who would be taking his leave. One of the two leather bags that sat at his feet contained his clothes and other necessary belongings, while the second smaller and heavier contained books, paper, pens and all that he had been advised to bring to support his studying. The *Gymnasium* at Seddin was one of a few which had been set up as a preparatory secondary school, a college to prepare boys for entry to further study at university. Karl would be there for about five years, and he would be expected to pass the required annual exams, and then his final entrance papers which would, he hoped, gain him entry to a school in Berlin where a further two or three years of study would hopefully gain him entrance to the Friederich Wilhelm Institute of Medicine and Surgery to study medicine.

PART TWO

◆ ◆ ◆

CHAPTER TWELVE

1820-1825

At the *Gymnasium* in Seddin Karl had worked hard, applying himself to even greater efforts in the learning of mathematics, history and especially Greek. Here he was brushing shoulders with boys who were the sons of professional men, lesser civil servants and prosperous merchants. There were a few other boys from more humble backgrounds, but they rarely stayed on beyond age fourteen or so. Those aiming for higher office in the land would continue with their studies and, as Minister von Zedlitz had said, they would be 'exclusively schools for the noblemen, future officers, statesmen, scholars, preachers and doctors'. They were, by definition, men of intellect and spirit and bearers of culture suitable to fulfil their mission to become members of the Prussian state.

For Karl the next few years seem to pass in a flash. From his initial homesickness he soon found himself totally engrossed in learning new things and extending his academic skills under the tutelage of the masters. He returned in the summers to the little town of Ueckermünde but – did it seem smaller each time?

The townspeople he knew greeted him with the same warm informality – some more deferentially than others, unsure whether he would see himself above their station, but no – Karl was always happy to share a greeting and enquire after their health, or that of their mother, or child, or whatever. What saddened him was that sometimes these enquiries were met with a downcast look as they had sad news to impart about the demise of a loved one

– an elderly grandfather, a brother lost in a storm while at sea or, most heart-wrenching of all, an infant taken too soon from a doting first-time mother.

Johann delighted in the time they spent together in the *Apotheke* and Karl was eager to catch up on learning about the potions and remedies. The jars with the familiar names greeted him from their serried rows upon the dark wood shelves – *Aconitium, Folia Belladonnae, Nux Vomica, Ung. Gallae*, and so on. But it wasn't all work or study. Old boyhood friends soon tempted him out onto the Haff for a spot of fishing or birdwatching. The sandy stretches of coastline gave way to reed beds and amongst them, the wading birds made their nests and raised their young. Of course, as the years went on some of the lads were joining their fathers working the farms, taking their place in the shipbuilding trade or going out to sea, fishing. Others were taking up the trade of their forefathers – Friedrich for example was now following in his father's footsteps as a leatherworker, learning to make harness, saddles and bridles for the surrounding farm horses, as well as boots and shoes.

When Karl was fifteen, his uncle Otto asked him to come to their home in Berlin before travelling to Ueckermünde the following week for the winter break. By now, Otto had lost more hair but grown in girth and importance in his role as Supreme Court judge. As usual Aunt Ernestina fussed around the boy, while making sure that the maid was sent to supply coffee and cakes in the drawing room. Leading Karl aside, Otto gestured to his study and then closing the door behind them, asked Karl to sit in one of the chairs near his desk, which was overflowing with papers and documents.

"My dear nephew – as always we are delighted to have you stay with us for a few days. You will be wanting to return home before the weather turns worse, but before you do I have had a letter from your father in which he has asked me to have a talk with you."

"Is everything well at home?" Karl interjected, with a tremor in his voice.

Otto did not respond directly to that question, but instead held up his hand in a gesture signalling that Karl should be patient and let him continue.

"Your father and I are of the opinion that it is time to consider your future. Your time in Seddin will soon be coming to an end and we have to consider what you need to do next. I have been in touch with the *Direktor* of the school and he has given me an appraisal of your progress. How do you feel you are doing Karl?"

"Well Uncle, I have applied myself to my studies to the best of my abilities and so far have passed all my assessments, although I fear my mathematics is not as good as it might be. Is there a problem with this Uncle?"

Up till this point, Otto had not given any betrayal of his emotions, but now allowed himself a smile below his extensive greying moustache.

"Not at all, Karl. In fact *Herr Direktor* has praised your efforts and indeed, he is advising that you – we, now consider your next steps."

At this, Karl relaxed a little and wiped his sweating palms on his knees, allowing himself to sit back a little in the chair.

Otto continued, "And so it seems there are one or two options available to you. Have you any thoughts on the matter?"

Karl bit his lip and stared at his feet for a moment, then taking a deep breath replied, "As you know I have always wanted to go on to study medicine, Uncle. I do still very much want to become a doctor. The new Friedrich Wilhelm Institute in Berlin has a wonderful reputation and if I were able, I would wish to go there and study medicine. But ..."

And here Karl hesitated. Otto raised a questioning bushy grey eyebrow to encourage him to continue.

"Well, ... well I do not know if my father would be able to finance my studies further. I would not wish to burden him if it were to cause him any problems." And here Karl resumed his fascination with the spot on the wooden floor between his feet.

"Harrumph ..." responded Otto, while he continued to fix his eye on the boy. "Well, that is what we need to consider. Your father feels that he wishes to support you in every way possible and he has said that he wants you to go as far as you are able with your studies. There is a college in Berlin which prepares boys for the university examinations and will take only the best students. I have made enquiries and you may start there after the summer, provided that your *Arbitur* results are of the highest standard. Your father and I have come to an arrangement whereby we will support your studies ..."

At this Otto again raised his hand to quell any interruption from Karl.

"Provided you are willing to work hard, we are willing to support you in this. And your aunt and I are more than happy for you to stay with us while you undertake your studies. Our brood have mostly flown the nest, with only Emelie, our youngest unmarried and at home and her brother Alexander finishing his law studies. There is plenty of room for you at our home here at *Dorotheastrasse* and you will be able to travel daily to your studies. What do you say?"

Silence filled the small overstuffed room. Karl's attention continued to bore a hole in the spot between his feet. When eventually he lifted his eyes to look at his uncle there were tears.

"I would like it very much Uncle." Unable to say any more, he stood to shake his uncle's hand and received instead a bear hug and a hearty slap on his back.

Opening the door, it was obvious that Ernestina had been hovering nearby, aware of the conversation that would be taking place behind the dark and heavily panelled wooden door. Looking between the two of them for a clue to the outcome, her face quickly burst into a smile and she rushed over to hug her somewhat bewildered nephew.

"So it is settled ...?" she asked but with a note of delighted resignation rather than a question in her voice. She was answered with two heads nodding, and a growl of pleasure from her husband, followed by a request for coffee and cake – or maybe something stronger to toast the decision.

CHAPTER THIRTEEN

1825 – 1828

For the next three years Karl gave every waking hour to his studies, only returning home in the summer to spend the warm days relaxing in Ueckermünde or helping his father in the *Apotheke* or the Inn.

His final year at the college gave little opportunity for any diversions as he put all his efforts into his studies and making his father and uncle proud of him. Some might have called the boy unsociable, as he rarely joined in with the boisterous groups of boys who preferred to spend their evenings in the taverns of Berlin, or playing rough and tumble games in the *Tiergarten*, much to the annoyance of the older citizens. This was not what student life was about for Karl. His diffidence was often taken for rudeness and so he was not included in the antics, which often caused severe reprimands for other students. His entrance exams for the Friedrich Wilhelm Institute for Medicine and Surgery were looming and he was determined to do the very best he could.

But Ernestina could see that the boy was pale – and such a skinny lad! He locked himself away most evenings in his room on top floor of their three storey house, hardly coming down for meals. In fact, sometimes she had to send Maria up with a tray for fear the boy would go to bed having eaten nothing. Dark circles were beginning to appear under his eyes and often they hardly saw him for days, only aware of footsteps climbing the wooden staircase as he returned and went up to his room.

Alexander's studies were also coming to an end for the

summer break and so Ernestina drew her son aside one evening after their evening meal and had a word with him.

"Your cousin Karl is really worrying me. He is so thin and pale. He is working far too hard! You must see if you can get him out more. Can you encourage him to come with you and Emilie to the theatre some evening?"

"I can try mother," replied Alexander, who was a few years older than Karl, "but you know how determined he is. I'll have a word with him. In fact, I'll go up and speak to him now."

And with that, Alexander took the stairs two at a time and loped up to the landing where Karl's room was situated. Stopping outside his cousin's room, he hesitated, then knocked and entered. The room was quite small and apart from the bed, a wardrobe and a washstand with a pitcher and ewer on it, every other surface including the small desk by the window was covered with books and papers. An oil lamp flickered on the desk and another by the bedside, throwing shadows across the room. Karl looked up and smiled questioningly, turning his towards the door.

"Karl – you know it's really not good for you shutting yourself away all the time. Mama is getting quite concerned. I know ..." he paused as Karl tried to interrupt, "yes, your studies are important but there is more to life that studying. All work and no play makes Karl a dull boy! Look, I am going with Emilie to the theatre this Friday evening and I have a spare ticket. Come on, let's all go together. You will enjoy it, I promise you!"

"I need to pass these exams Alexander, you know that."

"And you will! No-one could have put more time and effort in than you! But you need a break – I promise you that you will be far better able to study after you have given yourself some time away from it all. I know – sometimes I get so bogged down I can hardly think straight. But I promise you, some time away from it makes it all the clearer when you return."

"Really? Well …"

"Good! That's settled then!" And with that Alexander slapped him on the shoulder and swept from the room, shouting over his shoulder, "We'll go for an early supper first and then on to the theatre. You'll love it, just you wait and see!"

CHAPTER FOURTEEN

1828

That summer was a glorious one. The crops ripened, the rain fell when needed and the sea gave up good catches of fish. And Karl gained entry to the Friedrich Wilhelm Institute for Medicine and Surgery. All the students were carefully selected and only the best would be accepted. And an added bonus was that, at the Charité Hospital which was the teaching hospital attached to the Institute, he would be given full support with his studies and paid a small stipend. He obtained almost full marks in his exams and with a huge sense of relief, began to relax a little with his cousins, enjoying some time in Berlin before making the two day coach trip back to Ueckermünde along the dusty rutted roads. The countryside became ever more familiar as the busy thoroughfares of Berlin and Potsdam gave way to the flatter landscape, mills and farmhouses of *Pommern*.

Now nineteen, Karl had become a tall and lanky lad, but already there were signs that he was beginning to fill out across the chest and shoulders. His mother soon vowed that she would be giving him a good feeding up and ... 'what was his Aunt Ernestina thinking of, letting him waste away like this!' He passed his days walking along the *Ueckestrasse* from the *Adler Apotheke* to the square which sat in the centre of the small town. There he would see familiar faces but some would pause and appraise him before recognising that it was Herr Kannenberg's young son.

Family outings to the dunes and the sandy beaches bordering the Haff were a great way for Karl to shed the pressures of study. Aunt Sophia would bring her children – now there were five of them – and they would laze on the warm sand or play in the shallow waters. A couple of the older children – Friedrich, now fifteen taking charge – would often take a boat out and try their hand at some fishing. As the days and weeks passed, Karl grew tanned and strong but never far from the back of his mind was the thought that ahead of him lay four long years of study, then practical medical training and then – who knows where he might end up?

His father, now in his mid-fifties, was still running the *Adler Apotheke* but Karl was dismayed to see that his father was looking stooped and tired, compared to the last time he had seen him at least six months ago. His breathing was laboured and he had to take a seat in between serving customers. His complexion was grey and drawn and his hands were starting to shake. He had also taken on an assistant, Georg Schallehn, who had come from Stralsund where his father was an apothecary there. This surprised Karl for he imagined his father would be able to continue on his own for a good many more years, but Georg seemed capable and willing to learn from the older man, as well as bringing some previous experience which eased the load on his father. Georg was required to complete seven years with a licensed apothecary and then complete a course in pharmacy and chemistry. Georg had done his time with his father in Stralsund but his older brother had started running the *Apotheke* there, so that was why he had come to Ueckermünde and it seemed Johann was finding him a capable and willing member of staff. Karl still lent a hand in the pharmacy, keeping his hand in at making up salves and concoctions, pills and remedies for the varied customers who came in search of relief from everything from blisters to colic, rashes to flatulence.

It was on one of these days, when the sky was uncharacteristically grey and the atmosphere humid and heavy with an impending storm, that the door burst open and a large gruff untidy man entered, shaking the first few raindrops from his cape.

"Kannenberg!" he bellowed, making the young messenger boy jump as he darted towards the door, pushing it closed against the rising wind.

"Dr Barthelt. What may I do for you?" Johann replied slowly, but still maintaining his usual pleasant manner.

"Need you to make up a tincture for a patient," and here he reeled off the ingredients he wished it to include.

"Of course, Herr Dr. When do you need it for?"

"Now of course, you idiot! I'm not going to come back again in this blasted weather!"

"I'm afraid it will take me some time to assemble the ingredients, and prepare and package it for you. It is not a common requirement so we only make it up to order. If you prefer, we can get it delivered to you later today?"

The doctor growled in response, sweeping past Karl and almost knocking him aside as he strode back over to the door, somewhat unsteadily. The pungent odour of stale sweat and some kind of alcoholic drink swept over Karl, causing him to look more closely at the man. Now well into his sixties, he guessed. And none to clean. There were grey greasy marks around his collar and cravat, his boots were dusty and his breeches spattered with dried remains of who knows what. Not a pleasant sight, especially for man of some standing in the community. He had known the man all his life – in fact it was Dr Barthelt who had been present at his birth and to whom he probably owed his life. What had happened to the man in the intervening years?

As the door slammed, causing the lids of the jars on the shelves to clink and clatter, Johann slowly walked behind the wooden counter, worn smooth with over 150 years of life in the old shop.

"What has happened to the man?" asked Karl. "He looks dreadful. He was never the most friendly of men, but …"

"I know Karl. He rarely comes here, preferring to go to the apothecary in Ferdinandshof, but he has probably been downing a glass or two in the Inn across the road after seeing a patient near here. Did you know that his wife died a few years ago? He takes very little care of himself now and it is obvious that drink has definitely got the better of him. I have thought of raising it with the town council but he comes here so infrequently that it seemed churlish of me to take such an action." And with that, Johann disappeared into the back room and began to assemble what he needed to prepare the order for Dr Barthelt.

CHAPTER FIFTEEN

1828

That summer seemed to pass so quickly and before long it was time for Karl to return to Berlin to continue his studies. His acceptance at the Friedrich Wilhelm Institute brought immense pleasure to his parents and it was with great pride that they stood outside the inn in late August as Karl prepared to board the coach to begin the journey back to Berlin. He had already discussed his concerns about his father's health with his mother and she too had expressed her worries to Karl, but not wishing to overburden him, had said that taking more rest and some of her good cooking would no doubt help. And Georg was able to share the duties in the shop. Karl's concerns were not so easily brushed aside and he had tried to allow his father to at least listen to his chest, but his hand was pushed away when he offered.

"A stubborn old man you have become Father!" he gently rebuked him, but nevertheless wished that he would take heed of the warning signs and accept some advice. The old man seemed to have faith in his remedies and was making up doses at the shop to ease his condition. Karl had caught him surreptitiously taking small doses of opiate, although he was unsure if his mother was aware of this.

Taking his leave of his parents in the early light of the morning, his eyes swept around the little town waking up to another day of work and business. From the harbour came the faint noise of hammering and sawing as the carpenters started work in the shipyards. Some of the stall holders in the market were beginning to set up for the day and the businesses which had shop buildings were starting to lay out their wares and pull back the shutters for another day's trading. At the far corner of the *Marketplatz* he could just see Franz Grossen getting ready for another day's business at his shoemaker's shop. And there was Friedrich, now fifteen lending a hand. Franz glanced up and raised a hand in acknowledgment and farewell, which Karl returned. Father of five children now, although they had lost two others in infancy, Franz worked hard to support his family and was now apprenticing Friedrich into the business.

The snorting of the horses, eager to be on their way, and the shouts of the stable boys in the Inn loading the bags, brought Karl's attention back to his parents. Charlotte had filled out over the years and there were threads of silver in her hair now, but her cheeks were as rosy and her eyes as alert as ever. Embracing them both in turn, he bade them farewell, his thoughts turning not only to the journey ahead, but also to the challenges he would be facing over the next four years of studying in Berlin. The journey would take a couple of days and necessitate changing coaches two or three times. A journey he had taken a few times now, but this time it seemed to be one which he felt he was more than ready to make. His other thoughts were about the next chance he would have to return to Ueckermünde, as his studies would continue through the winter and he would not be able to come back as often as he had in the past. And with that, a feeling of apprehension also crept over him as he looked at his father, stooped and slighter of figure than in the past.

CHAPTER SIXTEEN

1812 – 1829

While Karl was growing up and beginning his years of study, another family was also living their lives in Ueckermünde – and they were to play an integral part in Karl's future life. Gustav Sorge was a local Police Sergeant and spent his time divided between the city jail in the *Rathaus*, the Town Hall, situated in the centre of the town, and out and about in the small town, sorting out petty squabbles between neighbours, disputes over payment of bills from captains landing goods in the small port, catching stray dogs that were roaming the streets and becoming a nuisance, and generally being involved in the lives of the townspeople. He was well known to all, and his appearance at the end of the *Ueckerstrasse* would send groups of small boys scuttling out of sight, their guilty consciences pricking them about some small misdemeanour they had carried out, such as stealing apples from the trees in the orchard on the edge of the town, or tipping a basket of fish over the edge of the dock when it was being unloaded to pay back the surly captain who had clipped one of them over the ear when they had been jumping over the barrels and casks on the harbour side, causing a cascade as one toppled and fell, precipitating a domino effect and some foul language from the direction of the quayside inn.

Although not born in the town, Gustav Sorge had journeyed here with his young family in 1807. Stettin had suffered at the hands of the French troops, having surrendered ignominiously in 1806 when it appeared that the local Prussian troops would be outnumbered. The Mayor of the town offered the surrender, only to discover afterwards that the Prussian troops had actually outnumbered the French by about six times as many. The French troops would remain in the town until 1813. There were many great changes to take place in Pomerania over the next few years, and so it was that in early 1813 Gustav Sorge decided to take his young wife, and newly-born daughter Karoline, to a place he felt would be safer and more settled. Bundling up what they had, they travelled the sixty kilometres or so in a small cart. Heading north west towards the coast, and the relative safety of Prussian-held territory, the family were among others heading in the same direction and with the same purpose. Fortunately for the Sorge family, Gustav had a cousin, also serving in the police, and he had written letters to Gustav encouraging him to come to Ueckermünde where he would be sure of a place in the local force.

Gustav's family had found a place they felt safe, and began their lives in Ueckermünde in a couple of rooms in small house rented out to police officers, close to the *Rathaus*. In the following years the family grew, and they managed to find a house on the other side of the River Uecker, across the bridge, and there they thrived. Karoline attended the local school but by the age of ten, her education had effectively finished and she learned more about running a household and the duties of a housewife from her mother. As the oldest daughter, many of the day-to-day tasks fell to her. Taking the risen dough to the local *Backhaus* to be baked in time for the family to eat it, still warm, later in the day. Taking the younger ones to the school, and shopping for vegetables in the *Markt* on her return. She had little time to stand and stare at the groups of older boys who would pay tricks and run about the town noisily. But if she walked back home along the *Ueckerstrasse*, she passed the *Apotheke* of Herr Kannenberg, and would marvel at all the jars and pots to be seen on the shelves inside. And sometimes her eye would be caught by the sight of his young son who would be helping his father in the shop. He was a lanky youth, but at least he was not one to play pranks on unsuspecting girls, hurrying about their work! In fact, one time when she had been walking home in a hurry as the wind was whipping sleet up the road from the harbour, she literally ran into him as he came out of the shop heading for the Inn opposite. They both gasped and he had shot out a hand to steady her to stop her stumbling into the filthy slush of the street.

"*Danke schoen*!' she said breathlessly as she tried to regain her footing.

"You should have been looking where you were going!' he said somewhat accusingly.

"Well, so should you!" she said, her cheeks reddening with embarrassment and indignation.

Making sure that she had regained her balance, he let go of her arm and with a shrug of her shoulder and a flounce of her head, she pulled her woollen shawl tighter around her and set off towards home. But later she had thought about him again, and could not recall seeing him out and about much with the other groups of boys.

The second time their paths had crossed was when her father had badly hurt his hand on a large splinter of wood. The wound had become red and angry and was giving him a great deal of pain. Her mother had asked her to go to Herr Kannenberg at the *Apotheke* and ask for something to soothe the wound. By this time she was nearly sixteen and had grown tall, and her fair hair was wound round her head in plaits beneath her linen cap. She had come into the shop that summer day to be met with a stare from 'that boy' again – but he, too, had grown tall and was even showing signs of sprouting facial hair.

"We meet again", he said with a small bow of his head, "but I will try not to knock you over this time or gain your displeasure from any ill-thought-out words." There was a twinkle in his eyes as he smiled slowly.

Feeling her cheeks reddening, she hastily asked for something for her father's wound, answering his questions about how long he had had it, what it looked like and so on, before he handed her a small pot of salve which he assured her would help heal the wound and ease the pain.

After asking her name, he wrote something down in the huge ledger that sat on the desk, while she could hear his father in the workshop behind.

Looking for something to say, she asked him, "Are you going to be joining your father's business? I haven't seen you around very much."

After having explained that he had been at school in Seddin and then at college in Berlin, he told her was going to the Institute in Berlin after the summer to study medicine and become a doctor. And again she saw that twinkle in his eye, as he sounded so earnest.

"But," he continued, "I do hope I may have the chance to see more of you while I am here, before I go there in the autumn."

"Well, we'll see about that," she replied, "but you know where I live now so you *may* be passing by some time and I *may* be returning from the market or from buying fish at the harbour, and who knows – we might even 'bump into each other again'," she said with an impish grin which caused her nose to crinkle and with that she turned and left the shop, leaving behind a rather confused young Karl and a bemused Johann, who had heard it all from the back of the shop.

CHAPTER SEVENTEEN

1828 – 1829

Karl joined a large group of other young men at the Friedrich Wilhelm Institute of Medicine and Surgery in the autumn of that year. It was not a little daunting to meet the array of professors and tutors who would direct his learning in the coming months and years. Names he had only heard of were made manifest in ageing bombastic men whose method of instruction seemed to be bullying and belittling their students. Others seemed so mild mannered and vague that sometimes he wondered what on earth they had to impart – but when they did, he found himself hanging on their every word and marvelling at their wisdom. A few of the tutors had been Army surgeons and that was where they had learned their trade, and therefore their techniques mirrored experiences on the battlefield or in field hospitals. Speed was of the essence here and they were, by repute, men of skill.

That first half year of his studies covered lectures in osteology, splanchology – the study of the organs of the body, physics, pure mathematics, logic, and also studies of German and Latin. All his examinations would be taken in Latin and it was expected that he would have a thoroughly competent grounding in it. And also, most of the medical texts he studied were written in Latin. Karl was glad he had applied himself to his Latin and Greek studies so assiduously in the years at Seddin and with the *pfarrer* in Ueckermünde. How long ago that seemed now!

Karl most looked forward to lessons in the anatomy theatre when he took his place on the vertiginously ranked seating and looked down upon the arena strewn with sawdust, as the boisterous voices of the students became hushed when the body of some poor soul was wheeled in and the professor of anatomy started to impart the focus of the lecture. Up to 150 students would collectively lean forward as the attendants stood back and the imposing figure of Professor Rudolphus entered from the door to the side. Not unlike a theatrical performance and here was the main lead, the hero. Professor Rudolphus was the resident professor of anatomy and it was he and his colleague, Professor Knape, who would take these lectures. Such sessions were not for the fainthearted, but Karl overcame his initial feelings of nausea as he became fascinated with the sight of organs and muscles, systems that made up the working of the human body and which seemed to him, beautiful and utterly spellbinding. These were the lectures he raced to get as near the front as he could, the better to see and hear as much as possible.

The days were long, and Karl had little time for relaxation as his attendance at lectures started early in the day and went on till late in the evening. He had a room in a nearby building set aside for the medical students, which was just as well as oft-times he would be required to attend a lecture at six in the morning, and he would be seen sprinting across the grounds to the main building where lectures were held. One hand would be scraping his sleep-rumpled hair into some semblance of order while, in the other, he clutched the books and notes required for the day. And he would often stumble as he attempted to get a foot into one or other shoe, while trying not to lose a precious few seconds which stopping and doing so properly would have lost him. The days were long, and by the evening he would be eating alone while reading and then, as his eyes could no longer focus with exhaustion, he would fall into bed – often getting a meagre six hours sleep in twenty-four.

It had been decided that Karl would not return home that winter, not least because the days of travel in the foul weather of Baltic winters would take so long that he might not be able to get back before the next term began. Indeed there was but a minimal break before studies recommenced. In that small break Karl was able to visit his Uncle Otto and his family in their home in the *Dorotheastrasse*, and was glad to have a few days to enjoy the bright company of their grandchildren who were now filling their house for the Christmas celebrations. On the eve of Christmas, the family joined together and walked the few streets to the Evangelical church where they worshipped.

The Berlin winter was long and cold. Snow lay deeply in the streets and days were short and grey. Nightfall seemed to come before the day had barely lasted a few hours, and lights burned long in those months. Karl was introduced to the sight of the chemistry laboratory in that second session of his first year at the Institute. Here he was tutored in the reactions that the various chemicals would cause, and here Dr Turte would encourage a hands-on approach rather than one of lecturing at the students. For Karl it was quite familiar, as many of the chemicals had their origins in the materials in the jars within his father's shop, and handling tubes and vials came naturally. Some of the chemicals were highly dangerous and required the utmost care in handling. But with that came a respect for them, and understanding of their efficacy in various ailments and conditions. Hand in hand with these lectures were those of Dr Link on natural history, botany and toxicology. All of this would be integral to the drug dispensing physicians that they were being trained to become.

But what Karl most enjoyed were the sessions when the students visited real patients in the adjoining Charité hospital and were able to see medicine in action. Here the students were required to keep written records of their observations and even perform simple tasks at the bed-side. Using the tubular stethoscope he had bought on his enrolment to the Institute, Karl was fascinated to learn how to differentiate the sounds of an irregular heartbeat with that of a patient in heart failure. Here they were al-lowed to question the patient and from their responses, formulate ideas about the patient's condition.

CHAPTER EIGHTEEEN

1828/1829

The next term of Karl's studies in Berlin at the Institute and the Charité Hospital were once more marked by intense study and an exhausting schedule of lectures, assessments and practical sessions. Again Karl had a punishing schedule of rising early for lectures, while it was still dark and heavy frost lay on the ground, and late nights reading over his notes before collapsing, still dressed, onto his thin bed in his room while the candle burned itself out.

Again he did not travel back to Ueckermünde for the winter break, but joined Uncle Otto and Aunt Ernestina and their family. Having written a few letters to his parents to enquire after their health and to wish them well, as well as to update them of his studies and progress, he was always delighted to hear news from home. The town was thriving and especially the shipbuilding businesses. Having become the District capital in 1808, the town had grown in significance and importance. The Town Council took their duties very seriously and took great pains to keep detailed records of registrations required by the various trades within the town. Johann was expected to show that he was carrying out his duties as required as apothecary within the town, and Charlotte had hinted in her last letter that she was glad of the help he was getting from the assistant Schallehn, who was proving an asset to the business. The Inn was busier than ever and they had hired a manager to run the day to day business of the hostelry, while Charlotte still kept a keen eye on the accommodation side of the business. But reading between the lines, Karl was able to discern that perhaps his father was not as able as he had been, and coupled with the concerns he had had when he had been home last year, Karl began to feel uneasy about being so far away and unable to support his parents.

But soon his studies resumed and as Spring came to Berlin and the blossoms bloomed on the trees in the *Tiergarten*, Karl was once more engrossed in his studies. Karl's cousin Alexander graduated in Law and the family held a celebration in his honour at their home on the *Dorotheastrasse*. Karl allowed himself a night away from the Institute and enjoyed some family time with his cousins. Young Emilie had grown into a very attractive young woman and was catching the eye of quite a few admirers. But she had also discovered how to flirt, and many a young heart was going to be broken that summer.

Finishing his second year of study, Karl travelled the many kilometres north over the rutted roads to Ueckermünde, where he could not wait to see his parents again. As the coach came nearer the town from the south, he could make out the church tower of the *Marienkirche* and the imposing bulbous roof atop the hexagonal tower of the *Schloss*. A veritable forest of masts came into view as the quaysides of the town were crammed with sailing ships, and further away those being built could be seen. There was a hustle and bustle about the place with carts, horses and people cramming onto the bridge across the River Uecker, and the coach driver had to shout a warning as the coach carved a space through them.

His mother was waiting for him at the door of the Inn, a few strands of her greying hair escaping from her crisp linen cap. She seemed smaller, he thought, as he warmly embraced her and looked across the road to the *Adler Apotheke* to see if his father had heard the coach arrive.

"Come inside son," urged his mother, fussing over him and bustling him into the dark interior of the inn. Waving to a serving girl to bring some refreshments, she sat down at the nearest table, indicating to him to do the same.

"Where is father?" asked Karl, looking around and craning his neck to see through the open door towards the shop. His mother's face clouded somewhat, but she tried to hide the hint of a frown with some cheering words and grasped his hands in hers.

"He will see you soon," she said. "Oh, it is so good to have you home. You have grown so but, by the look of you, you need some feeding up!"

At this, the serving girl appeared with a couple of glasses and a brown earthenware pitcher of cool ale, a plate of bread and cheese and some small sweet cakes. Her eyes looked at Karl from beneath her lashes as she bobbed a curtsey and she was shooed away with a peremptory wave of Charlotte's hand.

"Mother?" enquired Karl, starting to feel uneasy.

"I will take you to him shortly," she said, "but first I have to warn you that he is not the man you remember. He has grown weary over the past few months and although he hides a lot from me, I know that he is not well and in some pain. He has been dosing himself but I fear that none of it is giving him any relief now. He has hardly been into the shop these last few weeks and has to go for a lie-down most afternoons. Indeed, even climbing the stairs is proving an effort for him now. I have to tell you this Karl, to prepare you for what you will see. But just having you back here will lift his spirits, I know it," she continued, a small smile returning to her lips although he could see tears in her eyes.

And indeed, Karl was heartbroken to see how frail his father had become – nearly nine months had passed since he had last seen him and the difference was marked. His hair was now completely grey, his cheeks seemed sunken and his complexion sallow. When he rose shakily to embrace his son, Karl could feel the old man's bones protruding through his homespun linen shirt. It seemed like a puff of wind could topple him and he was glad to lean heavily on his son's arm.

"Son – it is so good to see you and have you back home for a while. How are your studies going? How is Otto and the family? What have you been up to?"

Lowering himself to the couch, he gasped for breath, just the effort of those few sentences causing him to feel weak again. Karl sat alongside him and for the best part of the next hour, told him all about Berlin and answered all his questions. By then he could see that Johann was growing weary again and try as he might, his eyelids continued to droop every so often. Karl could not but help look at his father as he fell into any uneasy slumber, the rise and fall of his chest causing him some effort, and start to think of what might be the cause of his condition.

CHAPTER NINETEEN

1829

That summer was oppressive. There was hardly the faintest puff of wind, which usually blew strongly off the Haff, but now it seemed that the whole place was holding its breath. Crops struggled under the relentless heat of the sun, and the townspeople struggled under the effort of carrying on their day to day business with no respite, even at night time.

For Johann, the airless nights proved especially difficult and his breathing grew ever more laboured. Dr Barthelt was called but arrived late one afternoon, dishevelled and unsteady on his feet. He merely shook his head and gruffly said that there was nothing he could do.

"Had the man not already dosed himself? Anything I could prescribe would simply be the same."

Charlotte sat with Johann through another oppressive night, the small shuttered windows thrown wide admitting little moving air, merely the sounds and smells from the street below. Soothing his brow with damp cloths, she talked to him quietly and stroked his hand. Karl sat nearby and when his mother looked ready to drop, he took over and repeated the same duties, wishing there was more he could do. It seemed a very long night but just as the dawn crept into the room, Johann took a few final gasps and then was still. Charlotte and Karl held each other for a while, then Karl gently covered the face of his beloved father, as he held back the tears that pricked behind his eyes.

Shortly after that there was an enormous clap of thunder, followed a few seconds later by a flash of blinding light, causing them both to gasp as it startled them from their grief. A few moments passed and then the heavy plop of fat raindrops could be heard falling on the roof and onto the baked earth road below. In a few more minutes it had become a torrential downpour, and with it came a slight breeze and a cooling of the air – but too late to offer any relief to Johann.

Two days later friends and acquaintances gathered in the *Marienkirche* to say their farewells to Johann Karl-Alexander Kannenberg, town *Apotheke* and *Gastwirt.* He was only fifty-seven years old and according to Barthelt's registration of his death, its cause had been 'exhaustion'. The rain had fallen hardly without stopping for the last two days, and torrents ran down the town streets as they had made their way to the church.

Everyone had their own thoughts. Charlotte looked up at the white painted ceiling with its decorations and recalled their joy at standing side by side at Karl's baptism twenty years ago. Karl recalled the times he helped his father in the shop and how he always had encouraged and supported him in all he did. Sophia, Charlotte's sister, remembered her own marriage to Franz here with Charlotte and Johann by their side. The townspeople thought of a friend, a fellow businessman, a genial innkeeper, a strict record keeper and signatory on the Town Council. But they all knew that they would miss the company of a well-loved and respected citizen of the town.

As they slowly walked from the church after the service, the coffin being loaded onto the cart which would take it over the bridge and out of the town to the nearby cemetery, the rain stopped and the clouds parted for the first time in days, the sun shining weakly down on the bare heads of the congregation before their hats were replaced.

The women gathered around Charlotte and steered her back towards the Inn, while the men gathered around the cart and offered their support to Karl who had the lone task of accompanying his father on his final journey. Among those walking nearest him was Gustav Sorge, the town's Police Sergeant, and also Franz Grossen, Sophia's husband and Karl's uncle.

It was not an occasion that Karl wanted to remember, but that day it all seemed to pass so quickly and yet in such minute detail. The cart sliding in the mud and the horses straining to keep it on the track. The boots of the man in front of him becoming clagged with it. The grave with water lying in it and having to lower the coffin into it. The effort it took the gravediggers to heap the sodden soil back into the gaping hole. The journey back to the Inn that seemed to pass without him even noticing it.

Back at the Inn Karl went to his mother's side, her face drawn and her eyes still red and puffed from weeping. The first to come to offer their condolences was Karoline, and for a moment he did not recognise her, but then smiled weakly and accepted her kind words.

"Karoline has been a great help, Karl," his mother said weakly. "She has been helping me in the Inn these last few days. You remember her? The Police Sergeant's girl?"

"Of course, Mother. Thank you, Karoline. I am in your debt. With Sophia so busy with her young family, I am glad someone was able to offer my mother some female support at such a time, while I had to deal with other arrangements."

With that, Karl turned his attention to others in the dark and smoky room, and walked over to accept the sympathetic words of friends and citizens alike.

CHAPTER TWENTY

1829/1830

Karl stayed on into the early autumn until he was due to resume his studies in Berlin. He was torn about going back there and leaving his mother behind in Ueckermünde. But his mother waved aside all doubts and assured him that it was what his father would have wanted.

He saw more of Karoline as she, and her mother Maria, had become good friends to Charlotte, helping her through the next few weeks when Karl had been busy ensuring the shop would continue to run smoothly. Schallehn had proved more than capable, and Johann had left written instructions that he should take over the running over the shop in such circumstances, having a percentage of the earnings as his own, in return for providing income to continue to support Charlotte and Karl.

Karl discovered that Karoline had become a capable young woman, as well as a good friend to his mother and what was more, she had a ready wit and a bright mind. In conversations with Karl she could often turn a comment or better him at some logical response to a problem. She could be very serious, but then would burst into genuine laughter just as easily. She started to find a place in his heart.

But Berlin required all his time and energies.

Later that autumn, Karl returned to Berlin to start the

second year of his medical training. There was greater focus on Practical Anatomy and more lectures in the circular amphitheatre of the Theatre of Anatomy where he hung on the words of Professors Rudolphus and Knape. And now the students were allowed to have hands-on experience of dissecting various organs within cadavers, which the Institute procured for them. For some students this proved too challenging, and one or two left their studies to pursue another route, but not Karl. He was totally fascinated and spent many hours looking at the various textbooks in the Library or making drawings back in his room, as he memorised the fine networks of veins and arteries, marvelled at the attachments of ligaments and tendons and held in his hand the central organ of the body, the heart, with its muscular walls and delicate valves within the chambers.

Karl started to think about his father, and how he had felt so helpless at being unable to prevent his early death. He was beginning to have an appreciation of how the different systems of the body contributed to the well-being of the whole, and he gained some understanding of what the true cause of his father's death might have been. He strongly suspected some form of 'heart failure' and after one lecture, he pushed through the throng of students to the front of the hall and hovered near Dr Knape, who had just been giving a lecture about the interdependency of various internal organs. When eventually Karl did manage to have a chance to speak to the him, he felt unsure about how to begin. However, Knape waited while Karl began to tell him about his thoughts and then to ask his opinions on whether some form of 'heart failure' may have been the cause of Johann, his father's, demise. Knape seemed to sense that Karl was a young man of some worth and appeared to have some intuitive understanding, which was more than could be said of some of the students he had to work with. He gave him a few minutes of his time, briefly answering Karl's hesitant questions, then excused himself as he had another lecture to attend. But Knape had already seen something in the young man and, having asked his name, mentally marked him out worthy of notice in future lectures and tutorials.

Again Karl did not travel back to Ueckermünde over the winter break, but kept in touch with his mother through letters he scrawled when he could find some waking moments between lectures, studying and sleeping. It appeared that Schallehn was managing well in the *Apotheke* and that the Inn was also running smoothly. She asked after Otto and Ernestina and Karl was able to pass on her good wishes when he spent his usual Christmas break with the family at their home in the *Dorotheastrasse*.

The next term of Karl's second year at the Institute was similar to the first but there was the addition of a course of study of General Pathology. Here he met Dr Hufeland, who in 1828, as Dean of the Medical College, had integrated the Charité as a teaching hospital connected to the Institute. He also held the esteemed position of physician to the King. By now the doctor was in his late sixties, but as sprightly as a man of younger years. His lectures were inspiring, and he would often introduce more innovative ideas such as his views on the use of natural materials to treat ailments – what he called 'naturopathic medicine'. Not so different Karl thought, from the apothecary. He was also a supporter of '*homeopathy*' and '*macrobiotics*' – both terms which he introduced. He wrote 'A Treatise on Longevity' and recommended a vegetarian diet.

As the term was drawing to a close, and Karl had submitted his assessments for the year, his thoughts turned to travelling home and what he would find there. How different would it feel without his father to greet him and ask about what he had learned, the new ideas in Berlin and how his brother Otto was faring. It was with a sense of trepidation he stepped down from the coach at the end of a two day journey north to Ueckermünde, and seeing his mother waiting for him, arms outstretched in welcome, he could still not help but glance across the road at the *Apotheke*, half expecting his father to be at the door with his cheery smile.

The summer seemed to pass slowly, perhaps more slowly than usual, and he could not help but feel the days dragging with so little to do. His days at the Institute were so full that he barely had any time to himself, but here he seemed to have more time than he knew what to do with. He had brought some books with him so that he could continue his studies, but he spent much of the time on long walks along the Haff, having passed the shipbuilders hammering and sawing as they were racing to complete orders for more sailing ships. The town seemed to be a hive of industry and the shipbuilding trade had definitely grown, providing work and a good income for the townsfolk. As a result, there was a thriving market and money in the townsfolk's pockets to spend. New houses were being built on the outskirts of the town, which was now expanding beyond its mediaeval boundaries.

With more people and more money to spend, the Inn was doing a good trade, and another establishment had opened up nearer the port, which catered for the sailors landing their cargoes bound for elsewhere in the Pommern region – perhaps Berlin, Stettin or Thorn. An additional constable had been required for the Town Constabulary, and now Gustav Sorge had charge of a growing number of men to help keep order in the town. This consisted mainly of locking up rowdy drunks at the end of a day when they had received their pay after a long sea journey. But occasionally there were incidents of petty theft or disputes about bills.

Karoline Sorge was also looking forward to Karl's return. Now seventeen and growing into a pretty young woman, she had taken up a permanent position in the Inn with Charlotte, helping with the serving and maintaining the rooms.

"I could not have managed without Karoline," Charlotte confided in Karl, not long after his arrival. "She has been such a help and she is a delightful young girl. She often asks about you ..." She left the sentence hanging with a sideways glance at Karl. A slight nod and a raise of one eyebrow was as much of a reply as Karl was wont to give.

But it was not long before their paths crossed, and indeed with Karl staying at the Inn, they were soon in each other's company at some point each day. Her tinkling laugh could often be heard from downstairs, or perhaps he might hear her humming some tune to herself while making up a bed in a nearby guestroom. Sometimes, when the Inn was not busy, she would sit with Karl and ask him about Berlin – what was it like, how did people dress there, was the traffic really as busy as they said, had he been to the Theatre, the *Tiergarten*, ... and so on. Karl had to laugh as he tried to explain that his day to day life in the city was far from one of taking pleasures and relaxation. Although somewhat mollified by this reply, she still said how much she would love to go there one day – maybe she might even see the Palace – and perhaps the King and Queen in their fine carriage!

CHAPTER TWENTY-ONE

1830/1831

It was with a heavy heart that Karl left Ueckermünde in the Autumn of 1830 to begin his third year of studies in Berlin. Although his mother was coping well with the help of good friends and neighbours – and Karoline, he still worried that she must be missing the company of Johann, her partner and soulmate of all those years, taken so prematurely from her, so Karl felt, when he was not even sixty years old. But he took some comfort in the knowledge that the *Adler Apotheke* was running smoothly and that the Inn was also in good hands.

His third year of studies would cover some new areas – semiotics (the study of symbols), angiology (the study of diseases of the lymphatic and circulatory systems), syndesmology (the study of the ligaments), as well as other aspects of general medicine. Dr Schlemm gave lectures on the ligaments, their attachments and functions, and the students were encouraged to study these in closer detail while undertaking dissections of both animals and human cadavers. Dr Kluge also took a series of lectures and practical sessions on setting dislocated and broken bones, bandaging and plastering. Here the students would meet patients in the Charité Hospital and be expected to use some of their new-found skills on living patients.

As usual Karl's days were long and he threw himself into full-time study, barely leaving his room other than to attend lectures, sprint over to the Charité Hospital or visit a local *backerei* and take some bread back to his rooms for a late supper. He spent the winter break with

Otto and Ernestina again and was introduced to Alexander's fiancée, a young lady called Luise Schroeder. She was the daughter of a lawyer friend of Uncle Otto's and the couple planned to marry the coming summer. Meanwhile, cousin Emilie had grown into a young woman and would sometimes flirt a little with Karl, although he would laugh and call her 'my little cousin Emilie', much to her annoyance!

Some new topics were added to the curriculum in the summer term including surgery techniques from Doctors Kluge and Rust. Dr Rust lectured on some techniques he had used to rebuild the noses of patients whose features had been eaten away by the scourge of syphilis. And there were also lectures from Dr de Gräfe (the very one whose brother Johann had met all those years ago at the Inn), who had developed an innovative technique for palate surgery, which brought about great strides in the repair of cleft palates. Dr Kluge also delivered an intense series of lectures on pregnancy and birth, techniques for dealing with breech births and also the use of instruments to facilitate a positive outcome for mother and infant. Karl hung on every word of these esteemed and learned men. He found it profoundly moving witnessing a birth at the Charité, all the more so when it had been proving very difficult and the outcome could have been less than hopeful. A few days later, Karl was horrified to discover that even with the attendance of the best obstetricians in the land, and the care of the nursing staff, the mother had developed puerperal fever and died a few days later, leaving her babe an orphan. Although not uncommon, it still left Karl feeling angry and frustrated.

He found the lectures absorbing, as always, but he also spent some time studying the many gruesome exhibits and specimens in glass jars which were used to illustrate the various stages of foetal growth and development. There would be further lectures in the coming year about obstetrics, but the actual anatomy of the mother and foetus fascinated him.

Returning to Ueckermünde for his usual summer break, Karl found he was looking forward unexpectedly to seeing Karoline again – as well as, of course, his mother Charlotte. As the coach drew up outside the Inn and the dust from the horses' hooves settled, he jumped down, looking expectantly to see his mother waiting for him as she usually did, but he was somewhat perturbed to see that it was not her, but rather Karoline, coming through the archway from the inner courtyard, smiling and raising a hand in welcome.

She quickly reassured him that all was well in answer to his first question.

"Yes, your mother is perfectly well. She has gone to be with her sister, Sophia, who is very near her time ...," and at this her expression became more serious, "but come in and I'll get you something to eat and drink and you can tell me all your news."

Over some bread, a few thick slices of ham and pickled cabbage, some chunks of creamy cheese and a flagon of ale, Karl caught up with the situation with Sophia. This would be her sixth pregnancy and she was now forty-one years old. There had been a few years gap between this pregnancy and her last and indeed, the discovery that she was expecting again was a surprise to both her and Franz. But the pregnancy had been a difficult one, unlike her other ones. She had gone into labour in the early hours of yesterday and Justine Sollin, the local midwife who attended her other births, had been called and was with her now as usual. But it had been taking so long that Charlotte had gone to be with her earlier that day, when Sophia's husband Franz had come to fetch her at Sophia's request.

As the evening drew in, Karl could not help but think back to the specimens he had seen in the jars and the dissection he had witnessed of a pauper woman who had died in childbirth.

He would not be allowed to help, being unqualified, as there were strict rules and regulations about that, but he felt compelled to walk to Franz's house above the shop at the corner of the market square. Knocking at the now closed door of the shop, Karl looked upwards to the light burning in the window of the room at the top of the building. However, before the door was answered, he heard the arrival of horses' hooves and around the corner of the street came Dr Barthelt. Dismounting somewhat unsteadily, he grunted some indistinguishable words at Karl, and strode up to the shoemaker's door, as Karl moved aside. At that moment Franz opened it, and surprise registered on his face as he saw Karl, as well as Dr Barthelt.

However, Barthelt grunted, "Let me in man. Where is she – up here?" and brushing Franz aside, began to lumber up the stairs at the rear of the shop, grasping hold of a large battered leather bag.

"Karl! What are you doing here?" Franz had barely time to ask, before following Dr Barthelt upstairs. Karl could see the worry etched on Franz's face as turned away.

Knowing that he could not attend Sophia, Karl walked slowly into the shop and ambled about, idly picking up boots and shoes, hammers, pincers and nails, the tools of Franz's trade, all the time acutely aware of the sounds emanating from two floors above.

From the top of the stairs, Karl was aware of a face peering down at him – one of Sophia's children. Beckoning to him, Karl said quietly, "It's your cousin Karl. Come down and say hello."

The slight figure of Christian, barely four years old, came hesitantly down into the shop. His little face was ashen and he looked as if he might burst into tears at any moment.

For the next hour or so, Karl sat with Christian on his knee, telling him stories about the huge buildings in Berlin, the King's Palace, the twinkling lights of the theatres and the soldiers' horses marching in parades. Before long the child had fallen into a deep sleep, for which Karl was thankful. However, from above there still came no welcoming sound of a newborn's cry, only a lessening of Sophia's anguished screams, until these eventually ceased as well.

When silence fell, a huge sense of foreboding came over Karl. All could not be well. Footsteps on the bare wooden stairs made him look up but remain seated, for fear of waking the child on his lap. It was Justine, the midwife, a grey-haired woman in her sixties, short and stout. Her apron was blood-spattered although she balled it up from the hem and tucked it into her waistband when she saw Karl sitting in the gloom. She was about to make for the door to leave, but Karl called out to her, causing her to stop and face him.

"How is Aunt Sophia? Is the child born?"

Justine cast her eyes down and gloomily shook her head, some grey strands escaping from her linen cap.

"What has happened?" Karl asked, barely audibly.

"I'm so sorry, Master Kannenberg. Frau Grossen has died, and the babe never lived."

Karl sensed there was more she wished to say, and her hesitation portrayed an inner conflict. Karl tried to reassure her by asking her to tell him what had caused this to happen.

"I know I should not speak of this – but I have been delivering babes for nearly thirty years in this town and I have never seen such butchery!" Her voice rose and her cheeks reddened as her rage overcame her reticence.

"The babe would not be born and the lady could give no further effort. As you know, I can only do so much, so reluctantly Herr Grossen and I agreed to send for Dr Barthelt – that man!" – and here she spat contemptuously on the floor. She continued, having decided that now she had started, she wanted to make a full account of what had happened.

"Herr Doctor took command, not even taking off his filthy cloak or rolling up his grimy sleeves. Frau Grossen was exhausted and near to unconscious as it was. After a quick examination, he drew his forceps from his bag and, in my opinion, hauled the poor babe from its mother with no thought for the welfare of either. The child was already dead, I could tell, either from the effort of its birth or the brutal application of the forceps, but the Doctor's force caused the mother ..." and here she hesitated, either to draw breath, or else fearing she was saying too much and in too much detail.

"Go on," urged Karl. "I am training as a doctor in Berlin so I have some understanding of what you are talking about. You cannot shock me," he continued, but not feeling the certainty of that.

"... well, the sheer force of the extraction caused Frau Grossen to bleed profusely. Nothing we could do could stem it. She was so weak already that she had nothing left – and within minutes she had passed from this life and was gone." At that she made the sign of the cross, pulled her shawl around her head and made for the door as she caught sight of Dr Barthelt clomping down the stairs.

Karl was disgusted at the sight of the man. His father had been disquieted about the man's professional abilities – but had the council done anything in the intervening time? Obviously not, it appeared to Karl.

"Nothing could be done!" he growled to Karl, as he made for the door. "*Guten Abend*!", and slamming the door, he left the shop, having slapped a paper on the counter as he passed. His bill. Karl was dumbfounded. The inconsiderate behaviour of the man was unspeakable. This whole thing was wrong in so many ways. It should not have happened.

Christian began to stir and whimper as the slamming door awoke him. Franz came slowly downstairs and gently took the child from Karl's arms, burying his face into the child's neck as sobs broke from him.

Karl took his leave after his mother had come down and found him with Franz. She said she would stay with them that night, and Karl said he would return the next morning to help Franz make the necessary arrangements.

Karoline was shocked when Karl eventually returned to the Inn, just as the last customers were being urged to go home to waiting wives and mothers. Sitting together at a table, she poured a glass of spirits for Karl.

They sat for quite some time, talking about what had happened. Karl felt that the Town Council must now take action and remove Dr Barthelt from his duties by revoking his licence. When he did eventually lay his head on his pillow to sleep, thoughts whirled around his head with questions – what would I have done? Could I have done anything differently? Was there a better way? And so, a seed was planted …

CHAPTER TWENTY-TWO

1831 Summer

It was heart-breaking to watch as the funeral procession made its way from the *Marienkirche*, across the bridge and out to the graveyard, where a year before, almost to the day, Karl had buried his father. Franz stood at the graveside, with Karl beside him, as the coffin bearing his wife and also their stillborn child was lowered into the grave. The *pfarrer* said a few words of prayer and then the group of townspeople began to disperse, all men, and replacing their hats, started to make their way homeward. Franz hung back, reluctant to leave, but eventually he and Karl made their way back along the road together, leaving the gravediggers to their task.

Charlotte and Karoline were waiting on their return and as they entered the inn, Franz crumpled onto the nearest seat and buried his head in his hands. Charlotte had closed the inn that day and only family and close friends were there, as well as Franz's little family who were upstairs in the Kannenberg's living quarters. Friedrich was now eighteen years old, Henriette barely sixteen, then Ludwig who was thirteen, Dorothea just nine and little Christian, the youngest, at four years old.

Across Europe there were to be many funerals. But this time it was cholera which was sweeping relentlessly across from country to country, state to state, through cities, towns, villages and hamlets, no respecter of borders, city walls, rivers or seas. It took innocent lives and sinners indiscriminately with its cruel claws and left whole populations decimated in its wake. It appeared that it had started in India in 1826, then spread north and westwards through Russia and then across the rest of Europe. It reached Ueckermünde that summer in 1831. No-one knew who would be stricken down and who would survive. There had been such epidemics in the past and everyone knew they were right to fear its arrival, but seemed powerless to escape its hold, should they be chosen.

Even Karl's renowned professors could not be specific about its causes and prevention. All they could agree with certainty was its symptoms, its contagion and its deadly outcome.

In the weeks following Sophia's death, Franz kept the shop shut and seemed oblivious to the needs of his little family. In the end, although Friedrich and Henriette did their best to look after their younger siblings, Charlotte came to two decisions. The first was that she would take on looking after the Grossen family until Franz could resume their care and face making a life for them again. Friedrich did what he could in the shop, but once the remaining stock of boots and shoes was sold, he would only be able to undertake repairs as he had only partially learned his trade and served only part of his apprenticeship. He would have a few years more to do to complete this and enter into the guild of shoemakers, licensed to ply their trade.

The second decision Charlotte made was to take over the empty upper floors in the *Apotheke,* which were only being used as storerooms at present. Schallehn, who had taken over the running of the *Apotheke,* had completed his practical course in pharmacy and chemistry and was now licensed by the Town Council to practice as a fully-fledged apothecary in the town and surrounding area. Charlotte had drawn up a contract with him, whereby he would run the business and share an agreed percentage of the profits with her. He would be leasing the shop, while Charlotte would have use of the upper rooms in the remaining two storeys. In the last year, he had also become betrothed to a local girl, and they would be living in the house of her elderly mother, a widow, and the property would be left to the daughter in due course as there were no other siblings, so Schallehn had no need for the rooms above the *Apotheke*. Charlotte, now approaching her sixties, felt that she was ready to employ someone to take over the day to day running of the Inn, while she managed the household side of things to a lesser degree than before, but still had ownership and an agreed percentage of the Inn's profits.

When Charlotte first told Karl about her decision, he was initially taken aback that both businesses were effectively now not solely theirs, but he came to see that it was actually a wise move on his mother's part. And now, as she would need to help Franz with the children, it made eminently good sense.

But the nagging problem of Dr Barthelt still rankled with Karl. Over a tankard of ale one evening with Gustav Sorge, not long after Sophia's funeral, Karl was expressing his anger at the Doctor's lack of professional care, not to say, incompetence. Gustav agreed that together they should approach the Town officials, whose remit it was to renew the licence to practise for all medical personnel in the district. This included midwives, of which there were three (including Justine Sollin), apothecaries, barber surgeons (who mainly did bloodletting and tooth extractions, as well as barbering) and physicians – the latter group consisting of Dr Barthelt and also Dr Wahlstab, a surgeon from a military background, who mainly treated patients in the outlying areas. Having settled that they would approach the Council at the next opportunity they parted company, then Karoline cleared their table and sat in the chair opposite Karl, which had just been vacated by her father. The Council was due to meet in three days' time in the room in the *Rathaus* where they conducted their official business. But in the end, fate took a hand.

Gustav came into the Inn early the next morning and asked Karoline to fetch Karl down, as he wanted to talk to him. Sitting in a corner on one of the high-backed dark oak settles, the two men seemed to be deep in discussion as Karoline continued to wipe down the counter top and bring in some kindling needed for the fire later that day if the weather turned chilly. After a short while her father stood, the two men bade each other '*Guten Tag*,' and her father left with a smile and a wave in her direction.

Karoline had a fair idea what they had been talking about, as Karl had shared his thoughts with her the previous evening. He came and stood by the counter, shaking his head in disbelief.

"Well?" asked Karoline.

"You'll never guess. We have been saved the job of meeting with the council. Old Barthelt was found dead in a ditch this morning. A farmer and his son went out early with their cart and horse, preparing to start getting in the harvest, when they came upon a horse grazing on the verge, fully saddled and bridled. It was obvious its owner was not nearby, so the farmer tethered it to the cart and continued on his way. Some distance along the road he came upon what he thought was a pile of rags in a ditch, but on closer inspection he realised that there was a pair of boots sticking out of it. He dismounted – and found the doctor. He was stone cold and damp with dew, so he had probably been there all night."

At this Karoline gasped, but Karl continued.

"With some difficulty the farmer and his son managed to get the body onto the cart and they brought it into the police station about an hour ago. It didn't take long for someone to identify Barthelt – he's well enough known hereabouts after all. They sent for Dr Wahlstab to come to register the death and give a rough idea of the time it might have occurred. He confirmed it had been around midnight, and also that the man was stinking of drink. He concluded that he had fallen, or been thrown from his horse, and broken his neck in the fall."

"Well, I shouldn't say it I suppose – but he deserved it! God forgive me for speaking ill of the dead, but there are a few folk in early graves at his hand – and we know of one very close to our hearts."

Karl could only nod in agreement, while standing and making for the door in order to go and tell his mother and Franz.

CHAPTER TWENTY-THREE

1831/1832

As before, Karl returned to Berlin for his final year of studies in the early autumn of that year, 1831, leaving behind him a town fearful and in virtual lockdown as the dreaded cholera had arrived that summer and had already taken the lives of a number of its inhabitants.

At this time the cause was still largely unknown, but what was appreciated was that it spread quickly through a community, and that it was generally worse in hotter, summer weather. Close contact played a part but sometimes whole households would be struck down, while at other times only one or two of a family might sicken and die, or even none. Some would suffer with fever and the flux for days, while others would succumb within hours. No cure could be found and the only treatments and remedies that doctors and apothecaries could prescribe were those that reduced the fevers and stopped the bowels. Most people went out as little as possible, and the only movement on the streets was the women going early in the cool of the morning to the village well, or customers coming to the *Apotheke* for remedies. In the late evening another movement could be detected – the rumble of the cart coming to take the bodies of those who had succumbed that day to the graveyard out of town. Shutters would be closed and candles were lit early through those grim days.

Karl was loath to leave Ueckermünde, yet he knew that he must return for his final year of studying. At the back of his mind was the thought that he didn't know how many of his friends and neighbours would be there to greet him when he returned next year. And Berlin was also in the throes of the epidemic, so nowhere was safe, and he might as well throw himself into his studies and look to the future.

This would be the most intense year of his studies, for not only did he have to attend lectures and read up on the various topics, he had also to spend part of the year attending the wards and clinics at Charité hospital, which also made up part of his instruction. After these hospital sessions, he was expected to write up his notes from the scribbled jottings he made while on the wards and also, at the back of their minds, students were expected to begin to plan what their dissertations might be about.

When he returned to the Institute the first thing he noticed were that there were fewer students in his year group. Undoubtedly a few had dropped out over the years, but this was more concerning as these were students whose families, or perhaps themselves, had been stricken with cholera. There was a quieter than usual atmosphere as the students gathered for the first lecture of the new session, given by Dr Osann himself, Dean of the Faculty and esteemed physician and surgeon. While welcoming back those students who were in attendance, he urged them to remember those who had not returned – some who might at a later date, but many not at all. Urging them to be mindful of all that they had learned, he urged them to focus on the year ahead, the most testing time so far in their studies, and tasked them to remember in whose footsteps they were following, in the greatest profession that there could ever be – that of physicians to the people of Prussia. By the time he had finished addressing the students, he had somewhat roused their spirits, and it was with even greater determination that Karl set his sights on what he had always wanted to do in his life.

The first half of the year covered a series of tutorials and practical demonstrations by Dr Kluge on how to recognise the various types of fractures and also how to fix dislocations, for which they studied skeletons and occasionally, live patients at the Charité clinics. Doctors Rust and de Gräfe also gave lectures and practical sessions on surgery techniques and again, some of these were on live patients. These sessions were not for the fainthearted, and speed and skill were the two essentials, not to say also a confidence in one's own expertise, for patients were barely anaesthetised with strong gulps of alcoholic spirits, if at all, but usually, mercifully, passed out from the pain of the actual procedure. Amputations were particularly spectacular, requiring a team of four or five people. One or two of these might be required to hold the patient down, while, if it was a leg for example, the surgeon would swiftly take his large curved knife in a backward sweep behind the leg and around to the front, cutting skin and tissue as deeply as possible. Following that, he had but a short time to exchange the knife for a bone saw and, with the fewest and most forceful strokes possible, cut through the bone. By now blood loss and shock were the biggest enemies and once the bleeding could be staunched and sutures put into the remaining flap of skin, the rest was down to the Almighty whether the patient would recover or succumb. The most skilled surgeons boasted that this could be done in the space of two minutes – and indeed, it was not an idle boast for time was of the essence, and many of these men had honed their craft on the battlefield under fire and in some makeshift operating hut. It was breath-taking to watch and left the students in awe, almost certain that they could never achieve such a swift and sure technique – but most certainly, it was practice which would make perfect.

Karl returned to the Charité for another intense set of practical and theoretical lectures on birth and its complications. Here he became even more fascinated by the whole process and marvelled at how a woman's body could undergo such torment and yet, but a few hours later, she would be tranquil and able to move about unless there had been complications. He came to hugely admire Dr Kluge, who was the main tutor for the topic of obstetrics. More and more Karl came to ponder on the circumstances of Sophia's death and if it could have been prevented. Granted, the use of forceps was a tricky procedure, and not always ensuring the survival of both mother and child, but nevertheless it was his belief that more care and greater expertise would have saved either one or both of his cherished family members.

After a brief break over Christmas, Karl again spent some time with his Uncle and Aunt but for the last time in the *Dorotheastrasse*, as they were due to move in the spring to a new house in the *Wilhelmstrasse.* Karl resumed his studies for what would be his final term at the Institute. Everything he had learned thus far had to be revised and distilled into facts and diagrams that he could refer to in his final examinations. As before, these would be both written and oral, the latter in Latin under the fierce stares of three of the Institute's professors. Before that, he would have further intense clinico-medical practicals with Doctors Wolff, Bartels and Trustedt. He also took a short elective course of 'special therapy' and chose to observe Dr Jüngken in his ophthalmic clinics and take a block of his tutorial sessions.

But what Karl enjoyed most was the time in the Charité clinics, where he was allowed access to patients who had various ailments and had undergone, or were due to undergo, various major procedures. The Institute was a leader in encouraging the 'hands on' approach for medical students, and during each session students were expected to examine the patients, talk to them and question them about their symptoms and how they actually felt, take notes and give their diagnoses to the resident doctor in charge. Karl found this fascinating and came to realise how asking the right questions, not always the most obvious ones, would give clues to the cause of the patient's suffering and suggest the correct course of treatment. Many symptoms were, however, all too obvious. There were the cases of syphilis in the varying stages. Most often, patients whose faces had been eaten away by the filthy scourge were used to try out new and experimental treatments. In particular, having seen Dr Rust rebuilding syphilitic noses, he marvelled at the skills of Dr Dieffenbach, who carried out blood transfusions, pioneering skin transplantations and what would come to be called plastic surgery. (In fact, Dr Dieffenbach would become Director of the Institute in 1840.)

These were exciting times, were Karl to realise it, and many pioneering advances were to be made through the middle of that century. And Karl was just at the dawn of that age, perhaps aware with rising excitement, that there were some conditions and illnesses that could be successfully treated, or diseases whose causes might be identified and their fearful outcomes conquered.

Thankfully, by the late spring of 1832, letters from his mother had informed him that there had been no more cases of cholera in the town since February, there having been a harsh winter of hard frosts, deep snow and the river had been so ice bound that it was only by late March that boats were at last able to get in and out of the port area freely. Mercifully none of his immediate family had been affected, although it had been a testing time for Schallehn, the apothecary and the remaining doctor, Dr Wahlstab.

With his final examinations looming, Karl put all thoughts of home aside and focussed on his studies, his books and his written notes in preparation for the gruelling oral, written and practical examinations in May. He hardly slept or ate and spent long hours into the night at his studies. Occasionally he would walk through the darkened streets to the vast Charité hospital, its many windows shrouded with a few dim lights showing. The immense sprawling building covered a huge area with four storeyed buildings set at right angles to each other. The colonnaded front entrance was quiet and still at this time of night, but Karl would enter by a side door and would be greeted with a nod from the night porter who would recognise him as a frequent visitor. These nights he couldn't sleep until he had checked up on a particular patient he had seen over the previous days, perhaps one who was not doing well and whose condition had deteriorated, or a woman who had become ill with fever after giving birth a few days previously. His days were full and nights were long. It was just as well that Karl was a young and fit man of twenty-three, for tiredness often took hold and he would wake up slumped at his desk in his cramped little room, or in a chair by a bedside at the gentle touch of a nurse as the first grey light of dawn crept through the high windows of the hospital.

Karl gave every moment he could to studying and when the time came for his examinations, he gave his all. He could not say with confidence that he had done well, for the stern glances of the examiners gave nothing away. When he was finally dismissed from his last oral examination with a "*Vielen Dank Herr Kannenberg. Sie können jetzt gehen.* Thank you Herr Kannenberg. You may go now," he walked from the hall unsure whether he was relieved or terrified.

There was a general air of relief and a release of tension among the students who were in the same position as Karl, their four years of study complete, their examinations over and their results in the hands of the Gods. There were some high jinks in the streets of Berlin that evening as the students hit the bars and nightclubs of Berlin, determined to relax and have fun at last. Karl was swept along in the euphoria of the evening and woke up the next morning lying on the grass next to Fritz, a fellow medical student, as the sound of birdsong woke him. Leaning on each other's shoulders they made their way out of the *Tiergarten*, and along the *Unter der Linden*, each with a thumping headache and vowing never to do that again. On arrival at his student room he began packing in preparation for the coach trip later that morning north to Ueckermünde, and home.

CHAPTER TWENTY-FOUR

September 1832 - July 1833

Having caught up with family and friends over the summer months, Karl was feeling restless and much as he adored his mother and found himself looking forward to seeing Karoline, it felt strange not living at the Inn, but across the street above the *Adler Apotheke.*

Karoline was now nearly twenty-one years old and had grown into a capable and level-headed young woman, able to take charge at the Inn when Charlotte was not there and keep the household side of the business running smoothly. Sophia's oldest daughter, Henriette was now also working at the Inn, and Charlotte had engaged a man called Emil Benke, to take over the day to day running of the hostelry side of the business. He had lost his father in the cholera epidemic, and his sister Barbara, now widowed herself and left with two young children, was glad of the chance for her brother to be able to contribute to the family's income. Emil was a brewer on the outskirts of the town but had lost most of his men in the epidemic and so he had decided to move in with his sister. He usually supplied beer to the Inn, so Charlotte already knew him well and saw he was a trustworthy man and whose employment at the Inn would be of mutual benefit to them both.

Throughout those summer months, Karl found himself seeking out the company of Karoline more often. It was becoming obvious to everyone, if not to Karl, that the couple had a definite attraction. Karoline also enjoyed the times they had together, usually at a table in the Inn before it opened, or at the end of an evening when Karl would linger behind and help her clear up, then share a drink before bidding her goodnight. For the first time, he realised that he would miss her company very much when he returned to Berlin to continue his medical training.

It was at the end of a warm summer's evening as they were tidying up the Inn, that their conversation started to muse about what they would be doing in five years' time. Karoline laughed and said she would probably still be wiping down the tables here. Karl suggested that by then she might be betrothed, or even married with children of her own. Karoline's face clouded over and she sat down on the nearest chair.

"My father has been suggesting that it is time I settled down and he has already started looking round for suitable husbands for me. There are a few men in the area who have been widowed, and left with young children, and are looking for wives to take over running their households and looking after their young ones."

"And ...?" queried Karl.

"That's not what I want. Most of them are quite a bit older than me. I do not want to be mother to another woman's children. It's not what I want for my life, Karl. My father has not pressured me – yet, but I do feel he is getting a bit impatient with me as I keep putting him off and dodging the subject whenever it comes up. I can't just keep cleaning bar tables for the rest of my life!"

"I don't think that I want to see you cleaning bar tables for the rest of your life either Karoline." Karl paused, not really sure what he was trying to say.

He found himself stretching out across the table and taking hold of her hand. She looked directly at him, her blue eyes making contact with his deep brown ones.

"Karoline ...", he began tentatively. "Karoline, oh ... I don't know what I am trying to say but, well, I have suddenly realised how much I will miss you when I leave to go back to Berlin."

"Me too ...", she whispered. "You don't know how much I look forward to you coming home each summer."

"You have become a great friend to me Karoline. I know that my mother is in good hands with you by her side."

"Oh – so I'm just someone you can rely on to keep an eye on your mother and the family business!" At this, her cheeks coloured and she started to stand up, pushing the chair away from behind her with a scraping noise on the slate stone floor.

Realising that she had completely misunderstood what he was trying to say, he also stood and moved round the table in time to reach out and take hold of her arm, causing her to spin round to face him. Before they knew it, they were looking directly at each other and Karl could see how hurt she looked.

"Karoline ..." he began, but found he had no words. They stood for a few more seconds, looking at each other and then, without realising it, they were sharing a kiss. Pulling away slightly, Karoline looked up into his face and saw a smile creep over his lips, as she relaxed into his arms and allowed him to embrace her again.

His thoughts kept returning to his performance in his final exams and whether he would gain the marks required to continue his training. His time for learning was not yet over. He would have to return to Berlin to continue as a student doctor to gain the further experience required for his full registration, provided of course that he had qualified.

But before he returned to Berlin that autumn, he approached Gustav Sorge and formally requested Karoline's hand. It was an awkward conversation, for Karl realised that at that moment he had nothing to offer Karoline. And Gustav was impatient that she should settle down soon, for she was of an age when she should be starting her own family. There were plenty of men in the town who would be pleased to have her as their wife. Nevertheless, after consideration, Gustav said that he would agree to the betrothal, not least because Karoline had pleaded with him to allow it. He had a soft spot for his oldest daughter and he also admired Karl and in truth, was more than happy to allow the young couple to have his blessing. But they would have to wait until Karl's future was secure – and that meant he would have to leave for Berlin and continue his training.

Returning to the new rooms he had rented for the coming year, Karl unpacked his few belongings and set out his books and papers on the worn desk by the small window at the top of a four storey building near the hospital. A few days later, his results were posted in the entrance hall of the Institute on the first of October and Karl was relieved and amazed to find that he had passed all parts of his examinations – and with distinction.

Wanting to continue working in the Charité, Karl opted to work as a student doctor there, while also gaining evidence and practical illustrations to use as case studies for his dissertation which had to be presented in July the following year. Under Dr Kluge's watchful eye, Karl chose to take the subject of 'Puerperal Fever' as his topic, as he was more and more drawn to discover why some healthy women gave birth easily, with no complications, to healthy babies and yet would develop this cruel scourge and die within a few days.

Working long hours, the weeks and months passed quickly with Karl becoming ever more focussed on the women he observed in the maternity ward of the Charité. In the most part these were those from the poorest strata of society, often haggard, thin and filthy.

Working all through the winter and into the following year, Karl had little time for diversions, but when he could manage to do so, he would write to Charlotte and also to Karoline. There was little news of interest from home, other than things were going along much as normal. Ernst, one of the local bakers, had taken it badly that Karoline was now betrothed to Karl for he had hopes that he might marry her that autumn and she would be a new mother to his three young children, his wife and youngest child having been taken in the cholera epidemic. He had taken to drinking and more than once had to be walked home in a stupor from one or other of the town alehouses.

Karl's dissertation had to be presented in mid-July and as the date got nearer, Karl spent every waking hour either in the Charité or writing up his notes and researching information for his dissertation. He often visited the pharmacy in the hospital and studied the various remedies used for the women's treatment, bringing to mind the times with his father in the *Apotheke.*

The twenty-second day of July marked the date when Karl had to deliver his dissertation to the group of eminent professors who held his fate in their hands. He was shaking as he stood before them, but when he cleared his throat and began to speak in Latin, his voice soon became clear and firm as he delivered the words he had written and rehearsed so many times into the early hours of that morning. When eventually he concluded his paper, he was asked a series of searching questions by each of the assembled examiners.

An hour later, he packed up his few belongings and headed off to meet Alexander, his Berlin cousin, before catching the coach to Ueckermünde later that afternoon. Slapping him on the back, Alexander convinced him that a small drink was what was needed to restore his spirits and send him on his way. Toasting the end of this part of his training, they each downed a schnapps, then again toasted the arrival of Alexander's firstborn, Albert Otto Friedrich, born a few days earlier. Not surprisingly, Karl dozed for most of the journey north, only rousing himself to check in at a coaching inn, where he would spend the night before continuing his journey northwards in the morning.

CHAPTER TWENTY-FIVE

August 1833 onwards

It was a happy homecoming for Karl. His mother welcomed him with open arms, and this time there was someone else to embrace, although Karoline shyly put her arms around him and only allowed him to kiss her cheek while at the doorway of the Inn.

So much to talk about, news to impart about Alexander's new baby and Uncle Otto's even larger home in a better part of town. He didn't tell them much about the details of his hospital work but reading between the lines, they could see that he had worked himself hard in those last months, as he was pale and thin.

"We'll soon fatten him up," Charlotte winked at Karoline behind Karl's back.

Karoline smirked, " – and cheer him up!"

"Indeed!" was Charlotte's response as she busied herself with getting some food organised in the kitchen, leaving the two of them together in the back room of the Inn. It was only then that they could truly give each other the embrace they had wanted to earlier, and only pulled apart at the sound of Charlotte's footsteps coming back along the wooden floor of the corridor. Giving them a knowing look, she smiled and set down a large platter of cold meats, potatoes, vegetables and bread and went off to organise a flagon of ale to slake her son's thirst and welcome him home.

Although a shorter than usual visit home, Karl managed to have as much time as possible with Karoline.

Gustav was putting some pressure on the couple to finalise a date for their marriage but Karl wanted to be fully qualified and have his future assured before taking on a wife and all the responsibilities of a doctor. He didn't even know where he would get a position and if they would have to move away and settle, who knows where. Karoline accepted this and although she did not enjoy the idea of moving away from the town that had become home to her, she acknowledged that where Karl's work was, there would her life be, at his side.

Finding opportunities to be together whenever they could, they would enjoy picnics in the countryside. They would climb to the highest point in the somewhat flat landscape, the *Apothekerberg* or Apothecary Hill, with a view over the nearby mill and small farms, and the shimmer of blue in the distance marking the Haff. The little town could be marked out by the tower of the *Schloss* and the steeple of the *Marienkirche*. Already there were more houses spreading out into what had been wooded areas, now cleared and providing space for the building of homes for new citizens. The cholera epidemic had taken a fair few of the townspeople, but a booming shipbuilding industry was bringing in men keen to work and with that, came trading ships into the port. There was also a brickworks nearby and plans for another mill.

But all too soon, the time came for Karl to return to Berlin and it was a painful parting for them both. On his return he would soon discover if he had been awarded his qualification based on his dissertation. If he had, he had planned to work at the Charité as a student doctor for a further year to build up his surgical skills and gain more experience in all aspects of medicine. And he would also be earning some money, which he could now put towards his and Karoline's future together.

Again the months passed so quickly, and every day was an exhausting round of seeing patients, performing minor operations, and then ever more demanding ones, under the watchful eyes of the master surgeons at the Charité. Learning all the time and gaining experience in so many areas of medicine, Karl was proud to be working in the Charité, which was a shining example to the rest of Prussia, and indeed Europe, in the method of training doctors. Students came to study here from far beyond the kingdom's borders and doctors and professors visited to gain experience and information from the most eminent in the land.

Karl received his results a few weeks after his return to Berlin, when he was called to the office of his tutor and mentor, Dr Kluge. Sitting him down, the older man put his hands together, making a steeple of his fingertips as he exhaled deeply. In front of him was Karl's dissertation and alongside it some pages of scrawled notes in various hands. The silence stretched between them and further added to Karl's foreboding. Pursing his lips to consider how to begin, Kluge lifted his eyes to look directly at Karl.

"Harrumph!" he grunted, clearing his throat and taking a deep breath. "This is a fine piece of work Kannenberg. There are a few minor points I wish to discuss with you, but the remarks here from the other examiners echo my own thoughts and opinions. You may consider yourself now to have gained your medical degree."

At that Kluge sat back in his chair and continued watching Karl's reaction. As realisation dawned, Karl breathed in, finding he had been holding his breath in anticipation for some time.

"Thank you, Herr Doctor," was all he could say, as he allowed his face to relax and the hint of a smile to cross his lips.

The doctor leant forward, extending his hand, and gave him a strong handshake, offering his congratulations. They spent another half hour or so discussing Karl's future plans and courses open to him, as well as going over some minor points in his dissertation. Kluge felt that Karl was an all-round, able student and seemed to be capable in various areas of treatment. He had a good grasp and understanding of the various branches of medicine and specialisms. He could name any one of those in which Karl could continue and gain further experience and qualifications, if he so wished. This gave Karl some food for thought, but as he left Dr Kluge's office and walked along the long and echoing corridors of the Institute, he was turning over all the options in his mind. Did he want to continue with further years of studying? Did he wish to remain in Berlin? Or elsewhere? And what area of medicine spoke to him the most? In the end, he didn't have to think very hard about it. He knew what he wanted for the future ...

Karl worked on as a young doctor at the Charité for a further year and a half, honing his skills and focussing on what really interested him most. He wanted to focus on obstetrics. He was distraught when he saw how many poor women were lost through puerperal fever and how many came into the hospital, already having suffered at the hands of untrained hags out in the back streets. Some women were marked by the efforts to get rid of unwanted children through various methods, some more gruesome than others, which had given rise to complications, some of which brought about their collapse and soon after, their deaths. It was mainly those from impoverished backgrounds that found themselves at the Charité and Karl felt that their malnourished state and filthy surrounding must surely play a part in the outcome of their suffering.

Although he often found himself treating all manner of injuries, wounds, accidental or inflicted, he would find himself gravitating to the wards where the women in labour would be treated. Nothing gave him more joy than to help a woman give birth and then see her discharged a few days later, strong and well, with a healthy babe in her arms. Sadly this was not always the outcome and that distressed him more than he could say. Karl felt he owed it to these women to make sure they left clean and well kempt, and often would ensure that they had a warm shawl or a pair of boots from the donations to the poor, which the hospital would keep in a bank for this purpose.

CHAPTER TWENTY-SIX

1834-1835

Karl's graduation ceremony was to take place in the summer of 1835, but before then he made a trip home in the early spring to be with his family and consider his future. Travelling north along muddy roads and through driving rain was quite an effort for the coach and horses, but he arrived one gloomy grey afternoon in Ueckermünde and again his heart soared as the Inn came into view as they crossed over the bridge spanning the grey and surging river.

Bustling his mother inside from where she had stood waiting at the door of the inn, huddled in a cloak over her thick woollen skirt, with a shawl pulled tight around her head and shoulders, he was instantly glad to feel the warmth of the room and inhale the mixed aromas of ale, food and tobacco. At the sound of their arrival Karoline appeared from a doorway behind the counter, and rushing forward, gave him a hug as he swung her round in his embrace, her feet off the floor and her fair plaits coming loose from their pins around her head.

Over the next few days Karl allowed himself some walks around the town, talking with old friends and making the acquaintance of new residents. He visited Gustav Sorge, Karoline's father, at the jail which was attached to the *Rathaus*, and discussed how the town was faring and what had changed over the intervening year. Karl discovered that there had been a series of locum doctors covering the town's medical needs, but that none had decided to stay on, causing the Town Council some concerns, for only Dr Wahlstab from outside the town could be called on in times of emergency and he was not always available. Also they were now reduced to just two midwives, as old Christina Fischer had died and only Barbara Schallet and Justine Sollin were available to cater for the needs of the town's women, and neither of them was young. In addition, the town's population was expanding what with the shipbuilding, the brickworks and all the trades that were associated with them. And as these were heavy industries, there were more injuries and accidents, further straining the medical resources available to the town.

At the end of December, Karl sat down with Karoline by the dwindling embers of the fire in the bar of the Inn. They started talking about their plans, although Karoline was always a little nervous of the thought of leaving her home and family and starting up somewhere new. But with Karl at her side, she reassured herself, all would be well. She would be with him wherever their lives together took them. In the flickering light of the burned-down candles, Karl told her about his work at the Charité, the women he had worked with, the people he had treated and his discussion with Dr Kluge.

"He wants to go back to work in Berlin," thought Karoline to herself, with a flutter in her chest.

Karl carried on explaining about the areas of medicine that he really felt drawn to, and how he knew he could make a difference. What he needed was somewhere that needed him.

As he held her hands in his, she marvelled at hands that were so slim, with long fingers, could undertake some of the tasks he had told her about – and some he hadn't told her fully about, with all their gory detail.

"You know that my duty is to be at your side, wherever you are. That is the promise I have made to you now and will make in my vows at our wedding. What have you thought about doing?"

Then Karl started to put into words the thoughts that up till now had been mere musings, that hadn't really coalesced into plans or actions, but now the more he talked, the more he felt that this was what he wanted, what he needed to do and the way that he could provide for her and hopefully their family, in the coming years.

He finished up by saying, "So, as there seems to be a need for a physician here in Ueckermünde, I am going to apply to the Town Council and put myself forward for registration. I will formally graduate in January and with that qualification I can take my oath in front of the Council as doctor for the town, and also as an obstetrician – a midwife."

At this Karoline gasped. "Midwife? But ... you are a man!"

"I know – but this is the area of medicine I have found so fascinating. I can bring knowledge and new practices to the town. There is much I can teach the other midwives ..."

"If they will allow you!" snorted Karoline.

"And," continued Karl, "I will still be able to practise medicine, prescribe and do surgery, while also treating any women who have need of me." Adding, " I won't see another woman suffer the way that Aunt Sophia did at the hands of a butcher," and at this his face darkened.

"I understand," said Karoline quietly, and standing behind him and putting her arms around his shoulders, she buried her head into his neck and said quietly with a smile, “and we can live here in Ueckermünde.”

Having applied to the Ueckermünde District officials to be registered as a doctor, Karl returned to Berlin briefly in the late spring of 1835 for his graduation and a small celebration was held for him by Uncle Otto and Aunt Ernestina, with the close family members, young and old. Alexander was now father to two young children and Emelie was betrothed to Bruno Schultz, a young officer in the Cavalry. He was there, resplendent in his uniform and looked tall and erect beside the petite Emilie, hanging on his arm. The older siblings were also there with their children and altogether it made for a lovely occasion for Karl's last days in Berlin.

While visiting the various Doctors and Professors who had tutored him while in Berlin to give them his thanks and say his farewells, Karl received many good wishes and some advice as well. The doctor at the Charité offered him a place there, should he ever wish it, for the staff had a great respect for the young doctor and the nursing staff found him a pleasure to work with as he always had a kind word to say to them, or a word of thanks to acknowledge their duty of care.

Sitting in the coach, rattling its way north, Karl started to plan out how he would live in Ueckermünde. He would need to think about where he and Karoline would live after they married – the date had been set for October, when he would know if his application to practise as a doctor and surgeon in Ueckermünde had been granted. In the meantime he wanted to meet with the other medical men who covered the area and get to know them. One he already knew well was Dr Wahlstab, who had been serving the area since 1810 and was now almost seventy years old. But there were two other young men, one a barber surgeon and the other a young newly qualified doctor like himself, who had come as a locum and stayed nearer Neuwarp about twenty kilometres from Ueckermünde. And he would have to win over the midwives so that they would work with him, not resenting him as encroaching on their area of expertise. Indeed, he fully understood that some women in labour would still prefer a trusted midwife they had known all their lives, to a young unknown, male obstetrician. There were definitely going to be some challenges ahead.

CHAPTER TWENTY-SEVEN

Late spring to end of 1835

Over the next few months, Karl and Karoline started planning for their future. Charlotte had now been able to let Franz take over the care of his children again, and they had returned to their home over the shoemaker's shop on the corner of the *Markt.* Sophia had been gone for nearly four years now and Friedrich, the eldest boy, had turned twenty-two and was due to complete his seven years' apprenticeship and was courting a young girl, daughter of one of the barrel makers who lived near the quay. Henriette was twenty and working in the Inn permanently now. Ludwig was seventeen and beginning to chafe against the tight rein his father kept on him, announcing he was going to sea as soon as he turned eighteen and there was nothing his father could do about it. Dorothea was serving in the family shop and the youngest, Christian aged eight, was still at school.

Franz had been seen in the company of a local widow, Agatha, who had lost her husband in the cholera epidemic four years ago, and Charlotte would not have been surprised if they soon married and she became a mother for the younger children, having two young sons of her own aged six and four. Mutually beneficial, both sets of children would have a home with two parents to care for them, and Franz would have two stepsons to work in the business or to train to have their own businesses in due course, while Agatha would have the security of a roof over her head and a breadwinner for her and her children. They were not the first couple to have need of remarrying, and probably not the last.

As a result, Charlotte was rattling round the rooms above the *Apotheke* and Karl and Karoline had decided mutually that when they had a home of their own, she should come and live with them. The Inn was now run efficiently by the manager she had appointed and with Karoline and young Henriette working there, the family still had a presence there, as well as receiving a share of the Inn's profits.

That summer Karl met up with the three other medical people in the area. He found Dr Wahlstab, now nearly seventy, to be failing in body but still as sharp in mind as ever. He still used many of the old methods, which Karl privately dismissed, but he had a good standing among the local populus, some of them having known him all their lives, which counted for a lot with country folk.

Dr Ernst Leonhardt, the locum who had come to fill the void when Barthelt had died, was six years older than Karl and had also studied in Berlin, gaining his qualification in 1827. He was a general physician and lived near Neuwarp, which meant he could cover that area of the countryside. He was glad that Karl was going to be added to the medics in the area as he was often unable to attend those needing treatment in time, and apart from Wahlstab, no-one else was licensed to undertake certain treatments. He was interested to hear that Karl, as well as undertaking general medicine and surgery, was also qualified as an obstetrician and he wished him well with that, fully expecting him to have to overcome some prejudices among the women of the area and, not least of all, from the midwives who already attended those in childbirth in the town. They enjoyed a good discussion over a flagon of ale in a hostelry in Neuwarp, and struck up what was to become in time, a lasting friendship.

His next port of call was to Friedrich Alü, who was by

trade a barber-surgeon. He was about the same age as Karl and was following the trade of his father. Unlike Karl, he was limited to certain procedures – for example he could pull teeth or do blood-letting, but was not permitted to undertake any other surgical procedures or prescribe drugs. And of course, he could also cut hair and shave customers. His premises were on the corner of the *Bollwerk*, near the quay. A good position, for he would have the custom of many a crew member of the various ships that docked in the little port, as well as the townsfolk themselves. Karl's visit was a brief one, mainly just to inform him of his practice in the town as they would not be encroaching on each other's clientele.

And finally the challenge of getting the local midwives on his side. First he went in search of Justine Sollin, now in her late sixties. She remembered him fondly as a young lad around the town, and of course, from the dreadful incident with his aunt Sophia, when she had been appalled by Dr Barthelt's treatment of her. He found her at home in her little house, at the very end of the *Grabenstrasse*, near where the old town walls would have delineated the boundary of the town in times past. It had just two rooms, one she slept in and stored her meagre possessions, the other was both kitchen and living quarters. Sitting him down on a stool by the rough wooden table, she leant closer to hear what he was saying with her good ear.

After exchanging some pleasantries and answering her enquiries about his mother's health, he started to tell her about his decision to come and work as a doctor in the town. At this her face lit up and revealed a toothless grin, she leant back and slapped her hands on her thighs in delight. However, he then broached the subject of him being a qualified obstetrician and explaining that he would be attending women in labour and helping with the births.

Her face clouded over and she expressed her distaste at such new-fangled thinking. She was quite sure, she croaked, that the women would not want a man to attend them, that was the way it always was and that was the way it always would be! Karl was at pains to explain that he would not be taking away any of her income or her 'patients', and that he would only be treating those women who were experiencing difficult pregnancies or births. He didn't need to remind her, he said, about the treatment of his Aunt Sophia at the hands of Barthelt, did he? At this she sat back and considered his words. In the end, she offered him a compromise by saying that they could let the women choose who they wanted to attend them. If they wanted her support and expertise, she would be happy to supply it but if they asked for him, or indeed if she realised that the birth was beyond any help she could give, then she would be happy for him to be sent for. And they parted, albeit grudgingly by Justine, on reasonably good terms.

His final visit was to the other midwife – Barbara Schallet, slightly younger than Justine, a rotund bustling woman who had given birth to many children of her own, and was well liked by the townsfolk and country folk alike. Again he was received with courtesy, and not a little surprise, when he knocked on her stout wooden door set in the thick walls of her farmhouse on the outskirts of the town near the mill. And again he was met with the same reaction when he explained his plans for his practice. She was much more against his 'interference', as she put it, than Justine but when he told her the terms on which he had parted from Frau Sollin, she grudgingly agreed to follow the same line.

"We will see," was her parting shot as he bent to leave through the low doorway and bidding her '*Guten Tag*' he strode back down the slight hill to the town, nestling between the lush farmland, the woods and the sea with a bounce in his step and a sense of accomplishment.

The date for Karl and Karoline's wedding was to be the ninth of October and Charlotte was enjoying planning a wedding for the daughter she had never had, although she had to be careful not to tread on the toes of Karoline's own mother. It was agreed that they would have the after-wedding meal at the Inn and that Franz would act as supporter to Karl.

Karl had planned that they would start their married life in some of the rooms above the *Apotheke* but that soon, when he had built up a reputation in the town and been paid some fees for treating his patients, he would use the savings to start planning for them to have a place on the edge of the town, near the fresher air of the country.

The day for the wedding arrived and started with drizzle and grey clouds sitting over the town. Karoline was feeling sick with nerves and could eat nothing. Her younger sister was helping her pin up her fair hair, and her mother was putting the last stitches into a ribbon trim to go on a new dress in deep blue made of the finest woollen cloth, drawn in tightly at her waist and with a matching bodice cut low at the neck to show the fine linen chemise below, edged in picoted fine crocheted lace.

Arriving at the *Marienkirche* an hour later, she was relieved to see that the clouds were breaking although only weak sunlight filtered through the clouds, and a breeze had blown up from the north east bringing a chill wind sweeping across the Haff from the Baltic. Friends and family were already in the church, its doors thrown wide to welcome all. Leaning on her father's arm to steady her, she took a deep breath and clutching a small posy of late autumn blooms and foliage, she stepped forward with her father into the cool interior of the church. At the far end she could see the *pfarrer* standing by the pulpit steps, and the organ was wheezing out a hymn tune. Standing at the front, her eyes fixed on Karl who, at hearing the chatter of the congregation change in volume and the swish and rustle as heads turned, raised his eyes from his feet and turned to watch as his bride made her way forward to stand beside him. Looking at him shyly from below her lashes, she felt the warmth of his hand as he grasped her chilled one and taking a deep breath, looked into his deep brown eyes and returned his smile.

At the end of the ceremony, they walked out of the church together and laughed as they were greeted by the cheers and good wishes of their friends and family, and quite a few of the townsfolk who had come to have a look. With the wind now blowing more strongly, they were all eager to get back to the Inn for their wedding meal and take a break from the formalities of the occasion.

Walking the short distance up the *Ueckerstrasse* together, arm in arm, Karl turned to her and said, "*Guten Morgen Frau Kannenberg.*"

"*Danke mein Ehemann,*" she replied laughing with joy and relief. 'My husband' – what a lovely thing to be able to say, she thought as her heart leapt with joy.

The rest of the day seemed to pass so quickly with Charlotte and the Inn staff laying on a wonderful meal with many savoury and sweet dishes. Plenty of fresh fish, pork, sausages and ham, pickles and potatoes were soon enjoyed by all as the ale, wine and spirits flowed. The conversations became a little raucous as the younger men started swapping comments and ribald jokes, slapping

Karl on the back and exhorting him to have another drink.

Karoline's sisters and friends had redone her hair and soon she would be wearing it in the style becoming of a married woman, tucked under a fine linen cap. But for the moment it still had gay ribbons twined through it which flew out behind her as she and Karl were persuaded to dance to the fiddle player who struck up a fine jig, while the another played a flute and yet another beat out a rhythm on a drum.

Before long, the evening light had faded and night fell on the town. Karl led Karoline across the road to the *Apotheke* and with her giggles ringing out into the street, carried her up the stairs to the rooms that would be their married quarters for the foreseeable future.

Charlotte had helped make the rooms on the top floor into a home for them. There was a main room for living in, with a window that overlooked the street two floors below. In the centre were a table and two chairs, and in the corner a dark wood press with the top as a cupboard with two doors and a lower section with two large drawers, which Karoline had been filling with fresh linens, sweetened with bags of lavender, that she had been making over the many months leading up to her wedding. A few other items brightened the room, such as the rack which held a few plates, and a shelf on which Charlotte had thoughtfully put a vase filled with fresh flowers. By the window was a desk with a lamp where Karl could work, and a large carved chair which had been brought up from the shop below and was the one his father would sit in while waiting for customers. The bedroom was more sparsely furnished, containing a chest for clothes and a bed with a small washstand to the side, on which stood a jug and a bowl in blue and white pottery.

Carrying Karoline over the threshold, Karl kicked the door shut behind them and set her down, putting his arms around her slim waist. Karoline closed her eyes as Karl leant forward to kiss her and her heart soared with the thrill and pleasure at the thought of the life ahead of her as the wife of this wonderful man.

CHAPTER TWENTY-EIGHT

1836

Over the next few months Karl had to acquit himself as an able member of the medical profession but there was a requirement for him to take his oath before the Town Council and present his qualifications before he could undertake any medical procedures in the town and surrounding district.

Dressing in his smartest clothes, and wearing a stiff white collar, the latest fashion in Berlin these days, he donned a thick jacket, and over it a cloak and cramming a hat upon his head, braved the whirling snow that was falling onto the already deeply covered road outside. Clutched under his arm was a leather satchel containing all the papers he would need to present to the Town Council, sitting in the *Rathaus* this morning.

Crunching his way through the deep snow, he headed along the *Ueckerstrasse*, turning left before the bridge into the entrance courtyard of the *Rathaus*. Above him loomed the hexagonal tower, with its wooden roof, barely visible through the swirling snow. Striding through the arched gatehouse and into the inner courtyard, he climbed the three steps to the imposing wooden door and turned the large metal ring. Pushing against the door, he entered into the building, and paused to shake the snow from his hat and cloak, before a scrawny clerk came forward and took them from him, ushering him up a flight of stairs to a room above where he would present his credentials to the local Town councillors.

The clerk took his place at a desk in the far corner

of the room, where he settled himself and shuffled his papers, before sorting his writing equipment and looking up towards the men arranged behind a long worn desk. Greeted by the man in the centre, Karl sat in the chair facing them, as indicated by a sweep of the man's hand, and laid his satchel on the table. After having spread the relevant papers in front of them – his dissertation, his Vita and his medical qualification certificate, there was some general comments about recalling his father's place in the community, and also the need for more medical personnel for a town that was growing in size and spreading out into the surrounding countryside. While this was going on, the clerk was taking notes, the scratching of his pen punctuating the silences as one or other of the men looked at the documents Karl had brought.

Karl explained he wished to be an obstetrician – in fact he intended that this would be the main focus of his proposed practice in the district, but of course he would undertake other medical procedures as required. There were some raised eyebrows at this and the man to the furthest right leant over and muttered some gruff words to his colleagues.

Karl was asked to leave the room while the men had a discussion and so Karl stood in the chilly corridor, looking out over the buildings below him, snow piled upon the steep rooftops with their small raised edges to prevent it falling on the occupants below as they left their homes. They were made so steep so that there would not be too heavy a weight of snow accumulating upon the roof which might cause it to sag, or even collapse. Small windows punctuated the *fachwerk* walls of wood and plaster and even at this time of day, weak lights showed from inside many of them. Over the tops of the houses he could barely make out the river heading out towards the Haff, and on out to the Baltic, as the grey gloom seemed to stitch together the sky and the land, blurred by the flurries of snow.

Eventually the door opened and Karl was asked to return to the room by the scrawny clerk. Again he took his place in front of the men as the central figure leant forward to address him. It appeared that they were in agreement and they would be willing to appoint Karl as a physician in the town, although it was quite a new-fangled idea to have doctor who would specialise in the needs of women. Karl could see that the man to the far right was still grumbling under his breath, but a sharp look and a theatrical clearing of his throat from the man in the centre, silenced him.

"We are aware that here, we are somewhat behind the times, and thinking in Berlin is no doubt way ahead of us, however we do not want to be seen as a backwater and ewe wish to take the town forward, giving the townspeople the best care and attention they deserve. For this reason we are agreed that you will be sworn in today as obstetrician and doctor for the town of Ueckermünde."

Karl was then passed some paper and writing materials by the clerk and read out aloud what was written on it.

"In accordance with the decree of the Royal Government dated the 8th of the month, an appointment has been made with the practising doctor, Dr Kannenberg, for him to take the oath of duty as an obstetrician. The assigned has appeared and taken the oath as follows:"

Karl raised his hand, while reciting the oath written before him.

"Ich Karl Ludwig Wilhelm Kannenberg schwoere zu Gott dem Allmaechtigen einen leiblichen Eid nach ..."

"I, Karl Ludwig Wilhelm Kannenberg, swear an oath to God Almighty ...",

and here he laid his hand on the Bible laid in front of him, continuing,

"... to practice obstetrics and will treat anyone, regardless of status or wealth who requests my services; that I will carry out my duties willingly and tirelessly; that, should a case prove particularly difficult, I will not allow myself to take any rash decisions but consider the case carefully and carry out any actions to the best of my abilities; that I will adhere closely to all appropriate laws and act in the manner of the best, conscientious obstetrician, so help me God through His Son Jesus Christ, according to the rites of the Evangelical Church."

Karl leant forward, and signed his name below the document, "Dr Kannenberg".

The clerk stepped forward and added the words, "Licence issued in negotiations under the requirements set out by the Minister of Spiritual and Medical Affairs." And then he scrawled his name below as witness.

The gentlemen sat back in their seats as the man in the centre stood up and shook Karl's hand across the table.

With that, Karl collected his papers, returning them to the leather folder and, led by the clerk, made his way down the worn stone steps to the entrance where he collected his cloak and hat, and was shown out into the wintry winds.

Taking the steps up to the top floor of the *Apotheke* two at a time, Karl threw open the door to their rooms and held his arms wide open to embrace Karoline. Spinning her round, he announced that the Council had confirmed his appointment as doctor for the town *and* ratified his registration as an obstetrician. Dancing her through to the bedroom he allowed her to fall backwards on the bed as they collapsed together, their laughter and happy voices carrying down below to where Charlotte sat by the fire in her rooms, smiling at the joy and laughter that now filled this place.

"Oh Karl, that is wonderful! Now you can really start doing what you have always wanted, taking care of the people in this town and using your gifts to help them."

"I just wish Father was here to see it," he replied with a sigh, his voice growing quieter.

"I understand – but I'm sure he does know. And your mother is so very proud of you Karl, as am I."

Karl's face brightened and he looked down into her bright twinkling blue eyes and thought himself the luckiest man in Prussia.

"Did you have a job to persuade them to allow you to practise as an obstetrician?" she asked.

"I thought I was going to have a battle with one of them, you know – old crusty Zeigler, but luckily the others were more open-minded and after some discussion I was given their approbation."

"Well, it's just as well, for you may have need of that sooner than you think ..."

"Has someone been to ask for me? I did not see anyone coming to get me ..."

But he was cut short by the look in Karoline's eyes, and the coy grin that was slowly spreading across her face.

Karl looked at her with a frown, then his eyes widened

as he opened his mouth to stutter, ”Are you …?”

As Karoline slowly nodded her head, full realisation dawned on Karl. Whooping for joy he picked her off the bed and swung her round again, then standing close he kissed her with great tenderness.

“When?” he asked.

“In August I believe, but it is still early days,” she whispered in his ear, while stroking his hair and tucking a stray brown lock behind his ear. “With the grace of God, you will be a father soon, Herr Doctor.”

CHAPTER TWENTY-NINE

1836

That year was one of frustrations as well as successes for Karl. It was understandable that it would take some time to gain a name and reputation for himself in the town, but he needed to make an income and patients were still relatively few. Ernst Leonhardt would occasionally advise patients who lived nearer Ueckermünde to send for Dr Kannenberg, as travel was often a deciding factor in cases of injury, blood loss or other life threatening conditions.

Karl took a walk down to the dock area of the town, and further along to where the shipbuilders had their yards. Here squads of men worked long hours, plying the various crafts demanded in building wooden ships. Carpenters, ropemakers, coopers, sailmakers, chandlers and sawyers. And of course, there were always sailors landing goods as the ships docking here brought coal, cloth, spirits and many other goods into the town. Some goods would end up here, but a lot would continue their journey by road to Greifswald, Berlin and further inland. There was always bustle and noise emanating from the workshops and quayside, shouts from workers and sailors, hammering and sawing, the creak of the thick ropes as heavy pulleys drew up the sacks and barrels from the holds of the waiting ships moored alongside and landed them on the *Bollwerk* and the ever-present gulls, swooping and screeching on the scrounge for anything edible that had fallen onto the quayside or into the water.

It was a fresh spring April morning and Karl stood looking over the bridge where, had he but known it, his father had stood on that very day twenty-seven years before, awaiting news of Karl's birth. It was easy to spend much time watching all the action below, and further into the distance to peer through the tangle of masts, ropes and furled sails towards the estuary where the *Uecker* ran into the Haff. Beside him, two seagulls swooped and screeched overhead, marking where two small fishing boats below him were unloading the day's catch of herring.

A shout caught Karl's attention above the cacophony of all the other voices, crashing, hammering and creaking. Looking down, almost under the bridge, he could see three men rushing along the quayside to a spot by the stern of one of the fishing boats. More shouting and the men were leaning over, looking down into the grey water of the river. One tried to climb down, while others called for more help and fetched ropes, uncoiling them from where they lay on the cobbled quayside. Karl watched in gruesome fascination as eventually something was hauled up from between the side of the boat and the water. With horror, Karl realised it was a man, dripping and barely conscious.

He ran to the end of the bridge, and dashed down the wooden steps two at a time, arriving by the side of the boat, as the seamen laid the body of the man on the cobbles. As the water drained from his rough clothing, Karl could quickly see a pool of blood seeping onto the stones beneath him from the area of his thigh.

Pushing the burly men aside, he said," I'm Dr Kannenberg. Let me past."

The men grudgingly stood back and Karl knelt down beside the man, whose face was now turning grey, and a grimace of pain hit him as Karl started to try to get access to the wound through the thick trousers he wore. A sailor nearest him passed him a knife, with which he cut through the rough homespun cloth and revealed a bloody mass. It seemed that the leg was broken, probably in more than one place, and that one of the bones was protruding from the flesh. From the amount of blood pumping from the wound, it was almost certain that a main vessel had been ruptured. Grabbing a rope from the hand of one of the men, he tied it round the thigh as close to the groin as he could and using a nearby stick, twisted it to apply a tourniquet. Turning to the men, he shouted for one of them to run as fast as he could up the *Ueckerstrasse* to the *Apotheke* and get someone there to fetch his instruments and bag from his rooms upstairs.

It seemed like an age before the man returned with two bags which, thank God, he had already instructed Karoline to always leave by his desk, should they ever be needed quickly. Normally he would have had at least one of his bags with him, but as he had only been out for a stroll, he had not brought them with him. The other bag was heavier and contained various medical instruments, each carefully wrapped in clean cloth and laid through leather loops in a leather strip which could be rolled up and tied with a buckle, having a sturdy leather handle attached to the top. It was this he indicated first with a nod of his head, still holding on firmly to the tourniquet with one hand and pressing down hard on the wound with the other. Telling the man to open and unroll it, he then got the man nearest him to take over keeping pressure on the wound, while telling another to keep the tension on the tourniquet.

With his hands now free, he instructed the men to find a flat board they could lay him on and take him into the nearby quayside inn, where Karl commandeered three tables to be pushed together and the board laid upon them. He spent the next half hour or so, working on the injuries that the man had sustained. Using a few gulps of brandy to deaden the man's pain, and shoving a block of wood between the man's teeth to bite on, Karl straightened the limb and got the bones back into alignment. Thankfully the man quickly lapsed into unconsciousness with the pain. Then, pouring alcohol over the wound, he repaired what he could of the ruptured blood vessels and finally closed the wound with sutures. Applying clean bandages and then splinting the leg, he eventually finished and standing back, pushed the hair from his eyes and mopped the sweat from his brow with the back of his forearm. Only then could he take time to stand back and actually think about what he had done. He had not had time to consider what he should do – he had just done it, and he truly understood now the value of all his training and student experiences while at the Charité.

It appeared that the man had slipped on the greasy deck and toppled over the edge of the boat, into the gap between it and the dock. The boat had then rocked with the flow of the water, trapping him between the two. The leg had been crushed and there were possibly other internal injuries which Karl could not ascertain at the moment. Only time would tell.

Some of the crowd around him had dispersed when they could not stomach what he was doing, while others ghoulishly wanted to watch. Only then did he have time to turn to the innkeeper and apologise for taking over his inn so peremptorily. In response, the innkeeper thrust a glass of brandy into his hand and the man's friends muttered their grateful thanks to him. They offered to have a collection to pay for the doctor's time, but instead Karl had a thought that word of mouth would be worth more than any coin.

"Just think of me if you have any need of a physician. I live here in the town and have my qualifications from Berlin and my registration by the esteemed members of the Town Council and District officials."

One of the men, clutching his cap in his hands, agreed that there were always accidents in the dock area and that having a physician nearby would be useful. Not all were as life threatening as this one, but it would be good to know who to call – what was his name?

And so Karl introduced himself, just as a burly man in a formal coat arrived, causing the men nearby to stand back in deference.

"Why has work ceased?" he asked pompously.

One or two of the men ventured to tell him what had happened while his eyes swept round the inn, taking in the blood soaked floor, the soiled rags and the various bloodied instruments lying about, having finished their task.

"I would shake your hand Dr Kannenberg but ...," and here his eyes looked down at Karl's gory ones, with a distasteful scowl on his face.

"Indeed,' replied Karl. "Perhaps we may meet in better circumstances another time."

With that, the man left, after having told Karl that he was Herr Schoenberg, the owner of one of the shipbuilding yards.

And so it was that Karl had his first taste of surgery as the town's new physician. Word of mouth was a great advertiser and slowly Karl got more requests for treatments, none quite as dramatic as that one though. The man did recover, although he required some time to get his strength back. The loss of income hit his family hard, with a wife and five young children to support. His leg was always slightly twisted and he walked with a permanent limp. He was not fit enough to go out on the fishing boats anymore and ended up as town sweeper, employed by the town officials to keep the market and nearby streets free of refuse and filth. The town also paid him some small amount from the poor fund to keep the family from starving. Karl could not help but wonder if he had actually done the man a favour or not.

CHAPTER THIRTY

1836

Over the next few months word got round about the new Dr Kannenberg – especially around the dockyards. Karl was sent for a few times to treat work injuries – thankfully none as serious as the first but nevertheless, requiring his expertise – suturing a serious saw cut, removal of a large wooden splinter from an arm, amputation of two fingers when a hand was crushed under a hammer, and two stabbings, both the result of a brawl at the quayside inn when sailors, who had been paid off after landing their cargoes following a long voyage at sea, got into an intoxicated brawl.

He was also called to cases which were due to heart failure, pneumonia in elderly bedridden patients and extreme vomiting in children. For some the prescriptions were simply to ease their suffering in their last hours, which always frustrated him as he could not do any more for them. Those tinctures and remedies that he prescribed would be made up at the *Apotheke* and collected or sent to the patients. Sadly, the drowning of a young boy was one case he could not treat, the result of two lads larking about on the bridge one evening. The youth was fished out by some sailors, roused by the other lad's cries, but by the time Karl arrived the lad was cold and blue. All Karl could do was confirm the death and send for the priest to inform the boy's family.

◆ ◆ ◆

It was stifling in their rooms at the top of the *Apotheke*, and now Karoline was near her time. Carrying anything up all the stairs became an onerous task and she wished they had a place of their own. Nearly three weeks into August, early one evening, she was bent over with the first sharp pains of her labour. Luckily Karl was with her and leading her to their bed, he assiduously piled pillows behind her and gently soothed her worries.

Charlotte went to fetch Karoline's mother, and when they both returned, she tactfully withdrew to her rooms below. Karoline's labour went on through that night and into the next morning. Karl was far more apprehensive, thinking how different when it was someone you knew and loved, instead of an anonymous patient at the Charité. Karoline was visibly scared but they both reassured her, her mother saying that she couldn't have a better person at her side than Karl. Eventually, as dusk fell that evening, Karoline's howls gave way to silence, and then the mewling cries of a newborn carried down to Charlotte below.

"Thanks be to *Gott*," she murmured and bowed her head in a silent prayer of thanks.

Karoline lay back on the pillows as her mother took the child from Karl and cleaned it, wrapping it tightly in a clean linen cloth. It had been a birth with no complications, putting to rest Karl's nightmares of the women he had treated in the Charité.

Handing the baby to Karoline she announced, "I have a beautiful little granddaughter. Congratulations to you both on your first born."

And so it was that Marie Charlotte Henriette came into the world on the twentieth of August 1836.

At the end of September, friends and family gathered in the *Marienkirche* for the baptism, with Franz and his new wife standing as godparents. Little Marie was strong and healthy, and every day Karl thanked God for his blessings.

CHAPTER THIRTY-ONE

1836 - 1837

The weeks turned into months, and soon Karl had been practising in the town for well over a year. He was regularly called to treat patients and attend accidents, either at the docks or at the surrounding farms.

One late spring afternoon, he was just returning home from a patient, walking along the *Bergstrasse* and turning left into the *Ueckerstrasse*, when he was approached by a young girl running towards him.

Gasping for breath, she asked if he was Herr Doctor Kannenberg, and then said Frau Sollin, the midwife had sent for him. The girl's mother needed his help as she had been in labour for nearly two days and at this the girl's face crumpled as she started to sob, saying that she feared her mother would die.

Karl stopped off briefly at the *Apotheke*, collecting his bag of instruments, and together they made their way through the *Markt* square, to the *Schweinemarkt* tucked into one corner, a short narrow street where the butchers plied their trade. Entering through a low doorway, he entered a dark cramped room and behind a curtain, another room was lit by one small candle. From here came the weak moans of a woman, obviously in labour. At his arrival Justine, the midwife, pushed the curtain back and explained that the baby was not making any more progress down the birth canal and that nothing she could do was helping the woman, who was now so weak that she feared for them both. Realising that this would be his baptism of fire, insomuch as this was his chance to prove himself to Justine, he took a deep breath, ignoring the foetid smells emanating from the squalid room, and followed her into the adjoining bedchamber. Seven pairs of eyes followed him, the butcher and his crowd of children, the oldest being the girl who had come for him.

Having pushed aside the thin bedcoverings, he noted the woman's shallow breathing and how clammy and grey her face was. Taking her limp wrist between his fingers, her pulse was barely discernible. With each contraction she hardly had the strength to moan, even less push. After examining her, he called for the candle to be brought as close as possible so that he could see what he was doing. He realised that the foetus's head was barely showing, and asked Justine to encourage the woman to push with the next contractions. After observing the woman's feeble efforts for almost half an hour, it became evident that he would have to help the woman by using the forceps to deliver the child. Using them to cradle the head, he asked Justine to continue to urge the mother to push as much as she could. With the woman almost unconscious, he managed to free the head and after a pause, the child was soon delivered. But it was crumpled, blue and not breathing. Holding it upside down by its feet, Karl tried to clear the airways, then laid it down to see if it would take a breath. Repeating this procedure with no success, he then began applying gentle massage to the baby's chest. Looking across at Justine who was shaking her head, he all but abandoned any hope when he thought he saw the merest movement of the baby's chest. Renewing his efforts, he was relieved to hear the first weak gurgle of it trying to take its first breath. Handing it into Justine's outstretched arms, he left her to maintain bringing colour back to its floppy body, while turning his attentions to the now collapsed woman. Applying some *sal volatile* under her nose, the woman started to stir and he turned his attention to ensuring that the afterbirth was successfully delivered.

He and Justine walked from the hovel as dusk fell over the little town and the last of the light silhouetted the town rooftops.

"Well, Dr Kannenberg, you have earned my respect. I did not think you would save either of them, but thanks be to God that you did. You were so gentle with the instruments you used, compared to that man Barthelt, God rest his soul, not wishing to speak ill of the dead," and here she briefly crossed herself. "I was sure that I would not be able to save the child and I feared that you would have to sacrifice it to save her. Mind you, another mouth to feed for them. They have lost two youngsters in the last few years – but we must hope and pray the Lord will look kindly on them."

At that, Justine bade him farewell and turned for her home, as he too turned his back on the setting sun and set off down the cobbles to the welcoming lights coming from the upper windows of the *Apotheke*.

It was another hot summer, which brought with it a threat greater than any war man could wage. Cholera was reported in Berlin and very soon, Karl heard of cases south of the town, and Leonhardt already had one in Neuwarp. Karl realised that if it were to enter the town, cases would quickly increase and they could face a major epidemic, especially being a port. Soon he had been called to two patients, both displaying symptoms consistent with the illness. Cramping of the abdomen, vomiting, purging of the bowels and discolouration of the skin, which was cold and clammy. One of these was a man called Peters, one of the crew of a cargo ship which had sailed from Hamburg, and he died within a few hours. The other was one of the police constables. Karl immediately contacted the Head of Police, voicing his concerns. The reply he received stated that he was sure the Doctor could deal with the two isolated cases and that he did not wish to cause panic amongst the townsfolk unnecessarily.

Karl wrote another letter stating, *"In the course of today, two cases of cholera came to me for treatment. Both cases died within a few hours. Although most of the symptoms displayed did not match those known as Asiatic cholera, but those of sporadic cholera, a danger of the spread of the disease remains. I do not wish to place blame – but this outbreak will cause alarm."*

The following day there were three further cases, again clustered around the dock area but naturally the crews had frequented the inns in the town and rubbed shoulders with dock workers, ship builders and citizens alike.

Not waiting for a reply this time, Karl strode into the *Rathaus* in person. He was assured his concerns would be passed to the relevant official but Karl was at pains to stress that they were of the utmost urgency.

Karl knew that if measures to protect the townspeople were not immediately put in place, the disease could get out of hand. Slamming the heavy wooden door behind him, he went round to the side where the town jail was situated, and where Gustav Sorge would, he hoped, be on duty.

Luckily he was, and having explained that time was of the essence, he tried to get Gustav to take some action, but he was loath to do so without the authority of his superiors, even though one of the victims was one of his own constables. In frustration, Karl demanded access to the cells. He would use the jail as quarantine quarters. Luckily there were no occupants that day. Gustav was shocked at such action and tried to dissuade Karl, but to no avail. Leaving the jail, Gustav went to try to get some authority from his superiors while Karl went round the town, to try to document how many suspected cases there were.

By that evening, Karl had arranged for three more sailors to be locked in the cells and no-one to be admitted, except for himself. In addition, he started to keep a register of households already beginning to be affected and the numbers of victims. It was the tenth of August.

Karl did not return home for the next few days until he had set up the jail as a quarantine facility. Each time he left, he posted the keys into a padlocked box at the *Rathaus* gate for which he was the only person with the key to unlock it. This way he kept the victims there in isolation, treating their symptoms as best he could. Other victims were still in their homes and the *Burgermeister* instructed the police to make sure everyone knew their families were to remain in their homes with them, only leaving if they had to get food. When Karl did go back home to briefly to collect clean clothes, he was careful to keep away from Karoline and baby Marie, now almost one year old. He made a decision then to push forward their plans for getting a home of their own, and on the outskirts of town where the air would be safe from the miasma of the crowded streets of the stifling town.

For the next few weeks, the town and much, if not all of Prussia and further afield into the rest of Europe, and eventually Great Britain, would be fighting the epidemic.

Karl assiduously kept a log of households affected. Ten days after the initial outbreak, the numbers in the town rose dramatically, then slowly subsided over the next four weeks. Karl kept the jail as a quarantine facility for those victims who had no homes in the town, while the rest were confined to their own premises. In the first two days he recorded four people falling ill, three dying and one surviving. Ten days later those numbers rose to twenty one ill, of which ten died. By the end of September sixty four people had fallen victim to the disease, thirty five had died and the rest had recovered. Karl had effectively reduced the spread of the disease but he still felt that he had failed, as so many had not been spared. Young and old alike were taken, although the very old and very young were worst affected. Thankfully Karoline and Marie were unharmed, but now Karl focussed on getting them a proper home of their own.

CHAPTER THIRTY-TWO

1837 – 1838

Over the next months Karl was kept busy with all the various requirements of a small town doctor. In addition, he had found a house on the *Kirchgasse* which ran north from the *Kirche* towards the bend of the river Uecker as it headed out to the Haff.

Karoline and Karl had decided that Charlotte should live with them. She was now in her sixties and visibly struggling to manage the one flight of stairs to her rooms in the *Apotheke*. When they put the proposition to her, she initially dismissed their suggestion, but when they explained that she would have no more stairs to climb and the air would be cleaner and fresher as the breeze blew off the Haff in the distance, she came to see that it would be a good move. In addition, Karoline announced in October that she was pregnant again and the thought of having a house full of grandchildren delighted Charlotte. However, she insisted that she would finance some of the work as she still had income from the Inn and the *Apotheke*. The rooms they had occupied would be rented out to Schallehn, whose new family was also outgrowing the house he had moved into with his wife's widowed mother. She had now sadly passed away in the epidemic and the offer of accommodation above his place of work suited him well.

Karl made sure the new house was sturdy and weather-proof and added extra rooms at right angles to the main building where he could have his study and consulting rooms, and where Charlotte would have her bedroom, separate from the main house but attached. It was a *fach-werkhaus* as was the traditional build of houses in that area. Strong wooden trusses supported the main frame of the building, and were covered in plaster, but the wooden framework still showed from the exterior.

As the cold northerly winds started to strip the last autumn leaves from the trees, the family moved into their new home. It was with great pride that Karoline was able to furnish the rooms as she wanted, but she always welcomed Charlotte into the large family kitchen with the cosy fire and together they would gossip and play with little Marie, while Karoline prepared their meals.

After a late spring started at last to bring some weak sunshine and warmer days, Karoline went into labour with her second child. It was a straightforward birth and although she was glad of Karl's support, his skills were not needed as both mother and baby were soon snuggled quietly among the covers on the bed, while Charlotte played with little Marie in the kitchen, sitting her on her knee and telling her stories.

Karl went through to them and, as his mother looked up at him enquiringly, he announced, "We have a new son! Ernst Karl Theodor – and what a fine healthy boy he is!"

Marie insisted that she wanted to see her Mamma and baby brother so they went through and found Karoline sitting propped up on the pillows with Ernst contentedly suckling at her breast. Karl felt his happiness was complete.

That year also marked Karl's official registration as District, as well as Town Doctor, which gave him great pride – and he only wished his father was here to see it. His standing and reputation was growing and now that Dr Wahlstab had finally been unable to continue his practice due to his age and growing infirmities, Karl took over the majority of his cases.

CHAPTER THIRTY-THREE

· 1839 - 1846

Over the next few years Karl's family grew. There were moments of great happiness but also times of great sadness. Karoline's next pregnancy did not have the happy outcome they had all prayed for. After a long labour, the child only lived for a few minutes and nothing Karl could do revived the tiny babe. It was a terrible blow to them all.

In November that year Karoline discovered she was once again expecting, and the following year she gave birth to another son on the eighth of June 1842, baptised Karl August. He was a very tiny baby, but he lived and was thoroughly cossetted by both Charlotte and Karoline. As time went on, Karl became concerned that baby August (as he was called) did not seem to thrive. He was often sick, and rarely kept a feed down. But slowly, with care and perseverance, Karoline managed to nurse the babe through those first few months, and eventually as the days shortened into winter, he began to fill out and look healthier.

Just over a year after baby August's arrival, Karoline gave birth to another daughter, Henriette Luise on the twenty-sixth of September 1843, thankfully a hale and healthy baby. But sadly she lost another child, as she miscarried in the September of the following year.

By now Charlotte was becoming quite infirm and Karl would prescribe tinctures and ointments to ease her stiff and aching joints. She was able to help less and less with the family, but the children loved to sit on her bed and listen to her tell them stories of when she was a girl and about their grandfather, the town apothecary.

Another son, Karl Robert (Robert as he would be known) was born on the twenty-eighth of October 1846, a large and boisterous baby, forever hungry and always demanding his mother's breast. But his birth was overshadowed by the sudden death of Charlotte, who gasped and collapsed one evening eight days later, as she was sitting telling the children their bedtime stories. Nothing Karl could do would revive her as her heart had simply given out. She was seventy-five years old and her life had been a full and happy one.

CHAPTER THIRTY-FOUR

1846 – 1849

Feeling suddenly very alone, as an only child inevitably does at the loss of the last of his parents, Karl found himself aimless and without focus for the days and weeks that followed Charlotte's death. Of an early evening, as the light was starting to fade, he would often ride out across the bridge to the cemetery and stand by the graveside of both parents, telling them about the children, how they were growing and what they were doing. It didn't take the pain away, but it helped to ease some of the emptiness he was feeling.

But life went on around him and time passed, gradually easing his pain and filling the void left by his mother. The children grew and demanded his attention, little sickly August always at the end of the line for attention, and only Henriette, his younger sister taking him by the hand and hauling him along with her to be enveloped in their father's arms. It saddened him to think of what future might lie ahead for the little lad, left out of the children's games as they raced down to the river to watch the ships or chase the squirrels through the trees in the birch copses. Instead he often just preferred to sit in their little garden consisting of a vegetable plot or two, some herbs for cooking and a low hedge of lavender for sweetening the linens and clothing. He was attuned to the songs of the birds and could already recognise a few by name and even mimic their trilling cadences, as his hearing seemed well attuned to the smallest of sounds, although Karl was at a loss to understand why August, of all his sons should be such a sickly child.

Karl worried that the boy would not be able to cope with approaching school days and all his hopes for his sons might have to be curtailed if August did not mature into a stronger boy, able to cope with the rough and tumble of school life. Ernst, the oldest boy, now ten years old, was already nearly finished his time at the local school, and plans would have to be made for his next steps.

The girls took after their mother with bright blue eyes and fair hair, while the boys were more like him with dark brown eyes and wavy brown hair. Sturdy little Robert was a determined toddler and always fought against being told what to do, often having tantrums and throwing his porridge on the floor and launching his spoon at Karoline, while now another son, Karl Gustav, was still a babe in arms having been born on the twenty-sixth of September 1848.

But for now, Karl had to focus on keeping abreast of the times and to that end, Uncle Otto would send him broadsheets from Berlin on the Post Coach once a week while he and Leonhardt, the other physician in Neuwarp would try to meet up occasionally and discuss cases and share what new medical discoveries were being made. Karl was astounded at the latest revelation by a Hungarian doctor called Semmelweis, working in Vienna, who was making a link between the deaths from puerperal fever and whether or not the women had given birth in a hospital. He proposed that he and the medical students carried 'cadaverous particles' on their hands and this was reported in a leading Austrian medical journal. As accounts of the dramatic reduction in mortality rates in Vienna were being circulated throughout Europe, Semmelweis had reason to expect that the chlorine washing of doctors' hands would be widely adopted, saving tens of thousands of lives. Sadly, there were many other medics who scoffed at the idea. But both Leonhardt and Karl considered that it was a possible way to prevent such deaths, although they were at a loss to understand why that should be.

Karoline fell pregnant again, just a few months after the birth of Gustav. With six children to care for, and now without their grandmother in the house to lend a hand, Karl hired a local girl to be a house servant and help Karoline with the daily round of household chores. Susann proved to be a capable and hardworking young girl, the children loved her, and she became a godsend to Karoline as she once more began to fill out through the spring and summer months of 1849. Karl turned forty that April and Karoline laughed as she spotted the first grey hairs appearing at his temples. They were a happy contented family; the children had their squabbles and sulks, but in the end they all liked nothing better than to gather together after the evening meal and sit by the fire while Karoline did some sewing and Karl smoked his pipe, a habit he had recently started. The children might sing some songs and the youngest would bang with a wooden spoon on a pan in an attempt to keep in time. August had a fine little voice and was quick to pick up a tune, so often he would take the lead and the others would join in. Sometimes the girls would take themselves off into a corner and play with their wooden dolls, usually making up illnesses that 'the doctor' would have to come to cure. Sometimes Ernst would come in late, having run an errand for Schallehn, now that he was an unofficial shop boy at the *Apotheke*. It made him feel important and he was proud to bring in a few *groschen* that he had earned to add to the pot.

At moments like these, Karoline would take a deep breath and allow her contented gaze to sweep over her little family and say a silent 'thank you' to God for her good fortune; everything was perfect.

That summer was very cool for a change, bringing squally winds and then violent storms blowing in from the Baltic. A frantic banging on their door one evening startled everyone as they sat around the large wooden table at their evening meal. Pushing back his chair, Karl went and opened the door to see a figure swathed in a cloak, glistening with raindrops that cascaded down its oily surface. Standing back to allow the man to enter, he quickly shut the door to keep out the chilly wind.

The man's gaze swept around the room, taking in the homely scene and he apologised for interrupting the family at such a time but he had been sent to fetch the doctor to Herr Schoenberg, the owner of one of the shipyards – in fact the man who had appeared when Karl had treated his first major injury all those years ago on the table in the quayside inn. The man said that Herr Schoenberg was in a state of collapse, had pains in his chest and was gasping for breath.

Gathering his bag and his heavy cloak, Karl pulled his hat firmly down and giving Karoline a quick kiss, said he would be back later. The man had come on horseback and said he would show Karl where to go, as Schoenberg's house was some way out of town, over the bridge towards Klockenberg. Saddling his own horse, Karl followed the man through the gloom as they made their way back through the town, their way lit intermittently by a pale moon every so often as the clouds swept across it and then parted.

When they eventually reached the grand house of Herr Schoenberg, Karl was ushered up a wide imposing staircase to an upper landing, and a door was pushed open by the manservant who then quietly closed it behind him.

Herr Schoenberg was in a large tester bed with his wife, Karl assumed, sitting on the edge and trying to calm him. The man was wheezing and was gasping for breath, holding his chest and hardly noticed Karl's arrival. Standing to one side, Frau Schoenberg allowed Karl to approach and make his examination. The man was clearly in pain, his face was contorted and his mouth drooped to one side. He barely noticed Karl through the one eyelid that was also drooping and barely open. His colour was ashen and he was cold and clammy. For the next hour or so, Karl did what he could do ease the man's agonies, giving him some opiates to calm him and also deaden the pain. But in the end, with a shudder and a slight gasp, Herr Schoenberg passed from this world.

Giving his condolences to the widow, and assurances that nothing could have been done for her husband, who had suffered from a massive failure of his heart and respiratory system, he took his leave with a small bow, collecting his hat and cloak from the man who had come to fetch him and had been waiting in the hallway below.

If anything, the wind was even wilder than before, the clouds whipping across the sky allowing the moon to be seen infrequently and for mere fleeting moments. The screech and howl of the wind unnerved his horse, and if he was honest, him also, but they headed back the way they had come, picking their way along and avoiding the thrashing branches from the wayside trees. Suddenly there was a sharp crack and a branch snapped and blew across their path, causing Karl's horse to rear and then stumble into the ditch at the side of the track. Karl was jerked sideways, then twisted and fell heavily onto his side, where he lay winded and bruised for several moments before he fully realised what had happened. Meanwhile his horse had made off in fright, in the direction of home, he imagined.

As he painfully struggled to roll onto his back, a sharp pain speared his chest and he gasped as his breath was torn from him. Clutching at his side, he tried more slowly to manoeuvre his legs to one side, get his elbows under him for support and ease himself to his feet, and again every breath seemed an agony. Eventually, by scuffling along on all fours towards a nearby tree trunk, and using it to help him balance, he managed to gain a semi-upright position. It took him some time before he felt he could get even the shallowest of breaths to allow him to actually try to make some forward movement. Yard by yard, he stumbled agonisingly in the direction of the bridge, eventually making out the sound of the river water swashing beneath the piers. Holding onto the rail, he inched his way along and each step brought a searing pain in his ribs and caused him to gasp and wince at every move. At long last he came in sight of the lights of the Inn and was spotted by two men, leaving it to hurry home, wrapping their coats tighter and hanging onto their hats. One stopped and turned a little, as his eye caught a movement, and then motioning to his friend to help, they ran towards Karl where he leant on the wall of the nearest building. With one supporting a shoulder each, they managed to help him stagger home.

It was a shocked Karoline who opened the door to them and with their help, got him to lie down on the wooden settle by the fireside. Thanking the men for their assistance, she tried to help him but was at a loss what to do for the best. He was obviously badly injured in the area of his ribs and was struggling to breathe. It would take hours to get help from Dr Leonhardt, especially in this storm, and the only other helper she could think of was Schallehn, the apothecary. Sending Ernst to fetch him, she knelt awkwardly by Karl's side, being impeded by her heavily swollen belly, and tried to get him to tell her what to do. His breaths were getting shallower and shallower, and his lips were turning blue. He was slipping from her, and there was nothing she could think of that would help him.

"It will be all right Karl. You will be all right. What can I do to help? I'm here," she repeated over and over, while praying that help would come soon. The children were ranged on the stairs, having been woken by the noise below, their eyes wide and only speaking in whispers.

"It's all right children. Your father will be fine," she said with more confidence in her voice than she felt. "Go back to bed. Susann – take them all back upstairs, then sit with them till Ernst comes back with Schallehn."

As she turned back to look at Karl, she was aware that he hardly saw her.

"Don't leave me," she whispered, stroking his head and tucking a wayward curl behind his ear.

But Karl left her, chilled and alone, as she knelt by his side in the flickering firelight of that August night.

By the time Schallehn arrived, he found Karoline and Marie rocking together in each other's arms as they wept heavy tears of loss. Ernst ran from the house, unable to face the scene in front of him.

The lives of their perfect little family had been shattered for ever.

A few days later Karoline went into premature labour, and was delivered of a tiny child, who took but the merest of breaths before being buried with its father in the cemetery, next to its grandparents.

Karoline was inconsolable from the loss of them both so close together, and felt she had lost her final link with Karl. Barely rising from her bed for the next few days, she only lifted her head when Susann brought the children in to see her. She could not imagine how she could continue without her beloved Karl.

CHAPTER THIRTY-FIVE

1850-1880

In time Karoline had to accept that she would have to singlehandedly raise her young family and take responsibility for their future, as Karl would have wanted and expected of her.

With her oldest daughter Marie by her side, they worked hard to keep the family together, and thankfully the money left to them in Charlotte's, and ultimately Karl's wills, meant that they were comfortably off. Karoline sold off the Inn and the *Adler Apotheke* in due course, although it was young August who liked to spend a lot of his time there. He loved watching the potions being mixed, and it would have pleased his grandfather Johann, if he could have seen him, to be so like his father when he had been a young boy at the apothecary's side. Schallehn's youngest son, Theo, became August's best friend and playmate, always looking out for him. Together they made plans that they would both study in Berlin together and become apothecaries.

Their oldest boy, Ernst, completed his schooling and at fifteen set out for Berlin to make his way, much to the sadness of Karoline. Thankfully Uncle Otto's oldest boy Alexander, now a lawyer in Berlin, let him stay with them and guided his steps. In due course, Ernst went into partnership with another young entrepreneur and they set up a coat and leather goods business in *Alte-Jacob Strasse* in Berlin. He married Therese Jess in Berlin and in the space of the following nine years, had five children, four of whom survived – Ernst, Hans, Elisabeth and Gertrud. In the early years of the new century, his eldest son Ernst would carry on the business into the 1930s.

In due course, against all the odds, August did go to study to be an apothecary, but while Theo came back to Ueckermünde to work in his father's *Apotheke*, August decided to stay in Berlin and after completing his registration period with an apothecary there, set up a shop on the *Friedrichstrasse* with a young Jewish chemist named Vielhauer. Around the first quarter of the new century, it probably changed hands but kept the same trading name, maybe passing to a son of Vielhauer. It branched out into supplying crystals and crystal radio sets and was still trading there under the same business name until 1939, when the Nazis closed down all business with Jewish connections. August never married and no date of death is known.

Henriette followed Ernst to Berlin and started working in his clothes shop. There she met a young man called Mierke and they were soon married. Tragically Mierke died, leaving Henriette a widow, and within a year she had also died, aged just 23.

Robert – the feisty headstrong boy has a story all of his own to tell – so dear reader, please bear with me and we will return to him in due course.

Gustav also went to Berlin in search of his fortune and set up business there. He married Marie Hille in Berlin in 1872 and over the next few years they had one son and two daughters. Gustav's great grandson would finally emigrate to Canada and continue the family line there.

By the time Karl and Karoline's brood had made lives for themselves, their oldest daughter Marie was well into middle age. On a visit to her brother in Berlin she met a widower, Julius Kedesdy, left with one teenage daughter.

He proposed marriage and they married in Berlin in 1871. Falling pregnant almost immediately, she sent for Karoline to live with them, as there were now none of her children living in Ueckermünde. Karoline was sad to leave the home that she and Karl had so lovingly created for themselves, but the thought of seeing her grandchildren, now all in Berlin, thrilled her, sweeping all her apprehensions aside. Sadly Marie lost her first child, but had two sons within the next three years. Karoline was once more in a house ringing with the sound of little children and could not be happier.

Walking slowly in the *Tiergarten*, leaning on the arm of one or other of her strapping sons, and surrounded by the grandchildren, of which there were now six, Karoline could not help but think of her beloved Karl and how proud he would be of them all. They had certainly had their tragedies, but there had also been successes and times of joy – she supposed just like any other family.

In 1880, after a stroll in the park on a spring day as the cherry blossom was fluttering down from the branches in the gentle wind, and the fresh green buds were appearing on the lime trees that lined the *Unter der Linden*, Karoline took to her rocking chair by the fire and nodding gently, quietly slipped away to join her beloved Karl.

PART 3

CHAPTER THIRTY-SIX

But let us return to one of the children – Karl Robert. He had been only two and a half years old when his father had so cruelly been taken from them. Eventually Schallehn, and later Dr Leonhardt, agreed that the most likely cause of his father's death had been a collapsed lung, caused by the broken ribs he had suffered in the fall from his horse that fateful night. Struggling to walk back home most likely exacerbated the trauma to his lungs as the splintered ends damaged a lung and caused it to collapse. By the time he had struggled to stagger home, it was unlikely anything anyone could have done would have saved his life.

Robert could remember virtually nothing of his father as the years passed. His mother and the older children would talk about him and recall happier times that they had spent together, but in truth Robert felt he had no guiding father figure to mark out his path in life for him.

He was always a strong willed boy from a very early age, and his mother and sisters despaired of ever taming his wilful moods and curbing his stormy temper. He was a short but strong little boy, with a stubby nose – "Like a potato", said his big sister Henriette, "stuck in the middle of your face!" and with that all the others would chant at him, "*Kartoffelnase*, potato nose!", which only served to anger him more, and then inevitably fists would fly, shins would be kicked and hair pulled, bringing their mother and Susann to try to quell the riot coming from the garden, or the kitchen, or the street outside.

He was not a good scholar either, and would often skip off school and sneak off down to the quayside, preferring to talk to the sailors and listen to their stories of far-off places. He didn't even seem to mind the beating he got from the schoolmaster when he was found out. His mother despaired of him, his siblings were always avoiding him for fear of being on the end of his temper and the townsfolk shook their heads and couldn't believe he was the son of the much revered Herr Dr Kannenberg, who had so tragically been taken from them.

As Robert reached his teens it became obvious he was not going to study further, and so his mother reluctantly agreed that he could get a job in one of the shipbuilding yards and arranged for him to take up an apprenticeship with the cooper, making barrels for the cargo ships.

But Robert was not one to bow to authority or follow instructions, and again he would slope off on sunny afternoons, down to the Haff with a fishing rod and sleep in the sun. The cooper eventually went to see *Wittwe* Kannenberg to complain that the boy was not following the terms of their agreement and that he was terminating the apprenticeship. Karoline wished Karl was here to talk some sense into the boy; nothing she said or did made one scrap of difference. His uncle Franz tried reasoning with him, his older brother Ernst, even the *pfarrer* and cousin Alexander in Berlin, but to no avail. He was simply a headstrong, stubborn lad, determined to do things his way and the devil take the consequences.

By the age of sixteen, he would often be found down at the inn by the quayside, drinking with the crews of the sailing ships newly berthed that day. And so it was inevitable that one day he came home to announce to the family, sitting round the table, that he was leaving home to go to sea. He had been taken on by the captain of a sailing ship bound for Nova Scotia and would be leaving on the evening tide the following day, by which time the ship's cargo would be loaded and supplies taken on board. His deep brown eyes twinkled with the thought of the adventures he would have, but his mother's blue eyes filled with tears at the thought of her son leaving home and facing unknown dangers somewhere across the world.

CHAPTER THIRTY-SEVEN

1862 onwards

Robert packed up his few belongings into a canvas bag, and after a hearty meal, at his mother's insistence, prepared to head off to the *Bollwerk*. Preferring to say his goodbyes at home, he took his leave of the family, giving his mother a brief embrace, and without looking back strode out of the door, and headed to the end of the *Kirchstrasse*, walked across the *Markt* square, then turned left into the *Ueckerstrasse*. With a brief glance up at the eagle statuette perched above the door of the *Adler Apotheke,* which gave it its name, he fixed his eyes on the end of the street where it crossed the bridge and headed out of town. Just as he prepared to turn sharply left and down the steps at the side of the bridge, he heard a voice shouting his name and the patter of running footsteps. Flinging his arms around Robert, his little brother Gustav implored him not to go.

But Robert disentangled himself from his grasp and told him curtly, "I am old enough to make my own way in life. I don't want to stay here for the rest of it! Just think of the places I'll see and the stories I can tell you when I come back. Now stop snivelling and let me go. I have to report to the First Mate and I don't want him to see me like this."

And with a shrug, he stood back from Gustav and with the merest of smiles, turned and jogged down the steps and was soon striding out along the quayside. The ship he was heading for was at the far end, making ready to finish loading and hoping to catch the tide as they would be heading out into the Haff and making for the Baltic later that evening. Soon Gustav couldn't make out the figure of his stocky brother, lost in the throng of busy sailors and dockworkers. Choking back tears, he realised that Robert hadn't even turned back to give him a parting wave.

As he walked along the cobbled stones of the quay-side and followed the curve of it as it turned north, he wouldn't admit that he felt any apprehension or sadness at leaving his home, or his youngest brother, so coldly. He wouldn't give heed to the little voice at the back of his mind which was trying to feed him doubts. This *was* what he wanted to do. This *was* the right decision. And sticking out his chin and drawing himself up as tall as he could, he walked up to the gangplank leading onto the ship he had signed up for. It was called the '*Adler*' which seemed appropriate and a good luck symbol given the coincidence, being the name of the *Apotheke*.

As dusk fell, the '*Adler*' headed out into the deeper water and turned her bow north, making for the *Stettiner Haff* and then the open sea. For Robert, the thrill of the movement under him, the creak of the ropes and shouts of the crew filled him anticipation, and before he had time to notice, only the *Schloss* tower and the spire of the *Marienkirche* could be seen in the growing dusk, as the little town disappeared from sight. But he had no time to admire the view as he was soon put to work, hauling on ropes and stowing items below.

The first few days of the voyage were reasonably calm, and Robert thought he must be a natural sailor, but as they made for the North Sea and the winds veered to the south west, he soon discovered that this was not the case. Amid laughs from the seasoned seamen, he clung to the rail of the deck and wondered what on earth he was doing here. After spending most of that night and the next day in his hammock in the cramped crew quarters below deck, he mercifully started to feel a little better and even feel some hunger pangs, having voided any stomach contents many hours before. Venturing up the steep ladder and onto the deck, he breathed in the fresh salty air which was a huge improvement on the stuffy noisome odours from the crew's quarters. One of the older sailors encouraged him to have some food, and from then on he felt much better and ready to face the trip ahead.

Calling in at Plymouth in England to offload and take on cargoes, he had his first glimpse of a foreign country, and on the quayside heard the incomprehensible words of another language. Feeling somewhat bewildered, he didn't venture far, although some of the crew made for the waterfront inns. He was put on watch that evening with an older seaman and was to make sure all the men returned and were accounted for, before they set sail in the early hours of the morning on the next tide.

Heading south west along the Channel, with a last look at land for some time, the dark shadow of the rocky coastline of the Lizard was the last thing he saw slipping from sight, as the dark waters of the Atlantic picked up the ship and fresh winds drove it forward, tugging at the sails and bidding it 'God Speed' on its journey to Nova Scotia.

About three weeks later, a voice from the crow's nest called out '*Land in Sicht*' and soon every pair of eyes was sweeping the horizon for the smudge of grey that would denote the shores of Nova Scotia. Coming into the harbour of Halifax, Robert was amazed at the hustle and bustle, the noise and the smells that assailed his senses after the weeks at sea. In those few weeks since he had left home, his hands had hardened through handling the rough salty ropes, and he had blisters and callouses to show for his pains. He had worked harder than he had ever worked in his life before, climbed rigging and learned knots and even some basic steering and use of sextant and compass to plot course and navigation. He may not have been much of a scholar before, but he thrilled at learning the techniques for reading the stars and plotting a course. It was as if it was something he had been born to.

Landing their barrels and nets containing their cargo of salt beef, flour, copper and tin took the best part of the day, and all hands were needed to pull their weight, but eventually the ship sat higher in the water and, with it firmly tied up at the quayside, the seamen looked forward eagerly to some time ashore. Naturally most of them headed for the taverns and less salubrious places to enjoy their night ashore, but Robert tagged along with the second mate – Gunther, who assured him that he wouldn't let any harm come to him, provided he was willing to enjoy a game of dice or two and have some fun in a local hostelry.

It was smoky, beery and noisy in the inn tucked up an alley that led from the quayside, redolent with the stench of fish and rope, and there Robert enjoyed a jug of ale with Gunther and began to relax, as a fiddle player struck up a familiar tune. There were quite a few German and Russian voices and Gunther told him that the crews all had their favourite places. The food was good here – great '*Wurst und Kartoffel*!'– and the innkeeper was himself of Prussian parentage. As Robert began to relax, two other men pulled up stools at their table and produced some dice. Robert had barely a coin to his name, so he sat back and enjoyed the atmosphere and the camaraderie.

Robert didn't remember much about that evening, nor how he got back to the ship. He woke up on the floor of the crew's quarters. Obviously the effort of getting into a hammock needed far more coordination than he could have summoned upon his return to the ship that night.

Robert was not too upset, therefore, when he was posted to stay aboard the next evening and maintain a part of the reduced crew required to stand watch. Even though they were in port, there was always at least one man on deck with a lantern to ensure no-one tried to get on board to steal anything. And also, one of the senior men would take a head count of crewmen returning, all the more important as they had a full morning of loading cargo the next day, before setting sail that afternoon.

Robert lost count of how many barrels of salt fish were loaded that morning, but put his back into hauling on the ropes and swinging the pulleys to lower them in nets into the hold, before the net would be emptied and the whole manoeuvre repeated again and again. He was becoming a strong young lad, and enjoyed the feeling of his muscles straining to the rope. A few other goods were hauled aboard, final checks were made and by the time the tide began to ebb, the '*Adler*' was already pushing out into the deeper water of the harbour and making for the open sea. Unfurling the sails, and now taking turns at climbing the rigging, Robert thrilled to the sound of the flap and crack as the wind caught hold of the canvas and he felt the surge of the ship as she drove forward as the helmsman swung the wheel to turn her bows onto the heading required to reach their next port of call.

They were bound for the port of Cadiz in southern Spain, where they would unload and then reload with a cargo of oranges and wine, before heading north again. They made the trip across the Atlantic in good time and arrived in the port of Cadiz just as the sun was rising over the red-roofed city.

Having unloaded their cargo at the quayside, which took most of that day, Robert was ready to explore beyond the dock area and was fascinated by the narrow streets, the whitewashed buildings with their tiny windows and the alleys that led him into the Cathedral square. The warmth of the sun was hypnotic, the light brighter and more dazzling than he had ever witnessed, making every colour sharper and more intense. Being a busy port, there were seaman of many nationalities and the hubbub of a dozen languages assailed his ears as he entered a taverna in the dock area of the town. There he met up with a couple of his shipmates and after enjoying some local food and drink, they set off back to the ship. One or two others of the crew headed for the narrow alleyways that led upwards from the quayside and winking at Robert, asked if he wanted to come along. Ribald laughter and a few digs in his ribs followed, but Robert decided that his hammock was a safer bet than a tumble with a Spanish 'lady'. Feeling his cheeks redden, he strode up the gangplank to the sanctuary of his place below decks, and thought about the stories he would have to tell when he got home.

A few days later, the '*Adler*' made her way out of the harbour and headed into the Atlantic, hugging the coast of Portugal as she headed north. The weather suddenly turned and they were hit with squalls of rain as the wind rose, blowing from the west and bringing dark grey clouds and churning the sea into a boiling thrashing maelstrom. The sails had to be hurriedly stowed, and Robert found himself equally thrilled and terrified as he hung onto the ropes and staggered across the decks, while the water washed over the gunwales and sloshed around his feet. Making a run for the shelter of Corunna, they hoped to take refuge from the storm. They were not the only ship making for the port, and some were already in such bad shape that they would be lucky to reach the harbour. With relief, the captain saw the outline of the fort at the breakwater marking the entrance to the harbour, and gratefully dropped anchor as he reached the calmer waters within the harbour walls. The storm raged on unabated for most of the next day, and it was only as dawn broke the day after, that the ship's carpenter and crew were able to undertake essential repairs to damaged spars and torn sails. Robert was detailed to splice frayed ropes and tidy the coils that had been tossed and tangled in the maelstrom.

Having lost a few days' sailing they were anxious to be on their way, briefly calling in to Bristol and unloading some of the oranges and wine they had loaded in Spain, and taking on board sugar, tobacco and coffee – products of the Americas now in demand in Prussia and the rest of Europe. Also loaded were bolts of woollen and cotton cloth in oilskin coverings, carefully stowed where they would be kept dry. Having entered the North Sea and struck out eastward for the entry into the Baltic, the weather turned perceptibly cooler and soon the chill winds from the wastes of Russia were heralding their arrival into the colder northern waters.

Their arrival in Ueckermünde both thrilled and saddened Robert. He had got a feel for the freedom of the sea, the dangers and delights of good and bad weather, the romance of far-off places and he dreaded the feeling of the restrictions of being in his home town with people that knew him and family who would try to map out his future. Hefting his canvas bag onto his shoulder and collecting his pay from the captain of the '*Adler*', he set off up the *Ueckerstrasse* and headed for home. The town seemed smaller and duller than he remembered, and only the odd nod of recognition from a few of the townsfolk marked his arrival. Taking a deep breath he headed down the *Kirchstrasse*, spotting his sister shaking out a rug at the door of their house and shooing away a dog that was sniffing at the gate. As she straightened up and made to turn towards the door, she looked down the road, squinting into the weak sunlight and shielding her eyes, then hesitated, trying to recognise the stocky figure approaching with the rolling gait of a sailor newly on dry land. Her hand flew to her mouth as Marie suddenly recognised her little brother.

Running to the gate to greet him, unconsciously smoothing her apron and stretching out her arms in welcome, she gave a squeal of delight.

“Robert! Look at you – so grown up! Mama will be so happy to see you!”

Feeling self-conscious at such an effusive display of affection in the street for all to see, Robert took her arms from around him and giving her a smile, headed for the open door. His mother was chopping vegetables at the kitchen table, helped by Susann and at first she was not sure who was silhouetted in the light of the doorway. As he walked forward, she dropped her knife and ran to envelop him in her arms.

“Robert! You’re home! When did you arrive? Are you well? Susann, look – it’s Robert!”

Later that evening, after he had unpacked his bag and handed out the small items he had managed to collect on his travels as little gifts for the family, they all sat round the fire as he told them of the marvellous sights he had seen, the storms and the seas they had come through, and the various nationalities of the people he had met. He entertained them with some of the foreign words he had picked up and, as they peeled the oranges he had brought back, they laughed as the juice ran down their chins. Only Marie, Henriette and Gustav were still at home. Ernst, his oldest brother, was now running a clothes business in Berlin and August was training as an apothecary, also in Berlin. Robert noted that no-one was calling him '*Kartoffelnase*' anymore.

At first Robert enjoyed the comfort of being part of a family again, but it wasn't long before his feet began to itch for the roll of a deck beneath them. He found himself feeling stifled and the walls seemed to encroach on him and squeeze the air out of him. He longed for the wide expanse of the sea, the hard labours that made him glad to roll into his hammock with aching muscles and fall instantly into a deep sleep. And – he admitted quietly to himself – the thrill and excitement of coming through the perilous storms, braving all that the elements could throw at them, and emerging victorious.

It wasn't long before he announced he was going back to sea. It was drawing him back and, knowing that there was nothing for him here in Ueckermünde, he would be signing on again soon for any captain who had need of a crewman with minimal experience. His mother's tears did nothing to dissuade him and it was a few days later that he came home from a visit to the quayside to announce that he had been taken on by the captain of another two-masted sailing ship, bound for England. This time he was not planning on a round trip and, with a tinge of sadness, knew in his heart that he would probably never be home again.

Over the next few years, Robert crossed the oceans many times and grew stronger, braver – indeed one might say foolhardier, for he had no fear of the raging seas and howling winds. He learned to handle the sailing ships that traded from one continent to another, and brought back goods to the ports of Europe and Britain. He worked for various ship owners under many different captains and mates, some better than others. He earned good wages, and spent a fair bit in the taverns and on the delights to be found in any port. Very occasionally he would think of his family at home, but never enjoying putting pen to paper, he always found he had something more pressing to do to avoid that task.

CHAPTER THIRTY-EIGHT

1870 onwards

By 1870 Robert had visited many ports and had many adventures. He was a sturdy muscular young man of twenty-four, not one to pick a fight with, as his temper was on a short fuse and he invariably came out the victor. He found Britain to his liking and found the temperament of the British people not unlike that of his Prussian countrymen. He would often sign on for shorter trips around the coast of Britain, taking goods in and out of the various ports – Bristol, Liverpool, Greenock, Belfast, Dover, Plymouth, Hull, Leith and so on. He picked up enough English to get by and undertake ship's duties, understand and give orders – albeit in a guttural and heavy Prussian accent.

One of his trips took him from Cardiff to Portaferry, on the entrance to Strangford Lough in Ireland, with a cargo of coal, a notoriously awkward cargo as it had to be stowed correctly and could move about in a storm, upsetting the trim of the ship and even endangering it in heavy seas. Piloting the ship into the harbour required a measure of skill as the tidal flow would cause a whirlpool effect and ships' captains had to know what they were doing to reach the quayside safely. There was many a shipwreck in the lough over the years and it took a skilled man to navigate its eccentricities. But the Master of the ship brought it successfully to shore and soon the dockers were unloading the cargo.

Hoping to sign onto another ship, Robert took a stroll through the harbour and gravitated to a tavern set back from the quayside. Laughter, and the sound of a fiddle being scraped in an Irish jig, drew him into the smoky interior and after ordering a tankard of ale he sat himself down in a corner and watched, bemused, at the antics of a couple of sailors and serving girls dancing and whirling in the space left in the centre of the room. Raucous shouts, hand clapping and thigh slapping kept the rhythm going, and soon Robert found his toes tapping along with the beat. When the music stopped there were cheers and whoops, soon followed by orders for more ale or Irish whiskey.

The low door opened and a man came in, wearing a dark coat and hat. Looking around, he made his way over to the corner where Robert sat and asked if he had just landed from the ship that brought in the load of coal. At Robert's nod, he asked if he might join him at the table, sitting down on the vacant chair. After ordering his drink, he engaged in conversation with Robert, just pleasantries about what his home port was and where he had just come from. He introduced himself as Joseph Gilmore, owner of the sailing ship 'Friends'. Robert estimated him to be in his mid-fifties by his greying hair and beard which, although bushy, was well trimmed and was complemented by a large moustache. He enquired about Robert's experience, and then said that the coal carrier's master had said that he might find someone to work at short notice, mentioning Robert Kannenberg by name. He was looking for a man to sail on her that evening, over to Girvan, to land some iron. After some more discussion about pay, Robert agreed to join the ship and with that, they shook hands and he was told to report to the ship's captain in an hour's time.

The trip over the Irish Sea was an uneventful one, and Robert soon found himself standing at the ship's rail looking out over the small Ayrshire port of Girvan. A few hours later, having unloaded their cargo, they set sail on the tide and were back in Portaferry by noon the following day. Gilmore was at the quayside as they tied up, and soon strode up the gangway and onto the ship. Talking to the Master, a man with a mop of sandy hair and a fearsome red beard, he glanced over at Robert, then resumed his conversation with the man. Eventually he walked from the bridge to the rail where Robert was stowing some rope, and asked him if he would be interested in signing on for another trip – just a short one this time, to take some foodstuffs and other sundry items to the small harbour town of Killyleagh, further north up the coast of Strangford Lough. With no other jobs in prospect, Robert agreed and that evening they sailed north hugging the coastline of the Lough, gleaming emerald green in the last rays of the sun.

Four other vessels were tied up at the pier in Killyleagh, and after carrying the sacks and small barrels ashore, Robert parted from the crew as they headed for their homes, all of the men being local to the village, or so it seemed. Strolling along the harbour path and heading up the incline into the town, he saw ahead of him a street lined with small shops, some just finishing their day's work and closing up. The town seemed to be well served by a variety of businesses, the streets were well kept and the roadway in good order. At the corner of the street he had walked up, he saw the lights of a small alehouse ahead and heard the hubbub of voices coming from within as the door opened and closed. As he entered, he was immediately engulfed in a fug of tobacco smoke and beer; the same the world over he mused.

After downing a welcome drink of the local porter, he struck up conversation with the innkeeper, a buxom woman of the name of Peggy, or so he thought, finding the accent a little curious to his ears. Enquiring if there was a bed to be had for the night, she said they didn't do accommodation, but some of the local people were happy to offer a bed for the night to ship's crew-members for a small cost.

Pointing to a ruddy-cheeked man at the end of the bar, she said, "Have a word with yer man Jimmy there. He usually has a spare bed." At which she bellowed, "Jimmy! Here's a man wanting a word wi' ye!"

At that, Jimmy slid up the bar to where Robert stood, and raised his brows enquiringly. "It's a bed for the night yer wantin'?" he asked.

"Indeed – if you have such a thing," replied Robert, at which the man appeared to have to process the words before making sense of them.

"Ah – I do, I do – a clean bed and a square meal for a shillin'."

"*Das ist gut*, thank you." Robert replied, smiling and taking the man's proffered hand in a firm handshake.

"So what d'ye be callin yerself then?"

Frowning for a moment, then understanding, Robert told him, "Karl Robert Kannenberg, but just call me Robert."

"Ye a sailor man then? Where are ye from?" asked Jimmy.

Robert tried his best to explain where Ueckermünde was but in the end they agreed that just Prussia would do, and that he spoke German, but could understand some English if it was spoken slowly.

As the landlady shouted at them all to be getting to

their homes, as she had a bed to get to, Jimmy led Robert up the continuation of the road he had come up, then turned right, then left bringing them into a street which ran parallel to the main street. This street was named Back Street, Jimmy informed Robert, and he could see it was lined with terraces of stone-built two-storey dwellings. Stopping at one a few doors up, Jimmy opened the worn wooden door and entered into a low-ceilinged room, lit only by the glow of the dying embers of a fire. Picking up a poker to stir the few embers, Jimmy lit a taper as the flames flared, and from it lit a candle on the table which was in the centre of the room. From the feeble light it shed, Robert could pick out a few chairs and a cooking range, a wall unit holding a rack of plates and a few other items of crockery. Drawing back a curtain, Jimmy showed him a small anteroom where there was a narrow metal bed, a small table and a stool. The bed was covered in a brightly coloured coverlet made from scraps of various fabrics sewn together and though small, the room and the rest of house, from what he could see, looked clean and reasonably well cared for. Bringing him the lit candle to put on the table, Jimmy wished him a good night's rest, and dropping the curtain, headed upstairs, his feet treading on the boards which creaked, then ceased, signalling his arrival in a room above. Robert thought he heard the murmuring of voices, then a few creaks and finally silence.

Throwing off his boots, and stowing his bag in the corner, Robert settled down on the bed, at which the frame groaned in protest but surrendered to his weight with no further objections. There was a clean linen cover on the thin pillow and under the coverlet, a thin woollen blanket and a homespun linen sheet. Pulling them up under his chin, and blowing out the candle, Robert soon surrendered to sleep.

CHAPTER THIRTY-NINE

The sound of someone moving on the other side of the curtain came through his sleep, and Robert realised that there was a glimmer of daylight coming beneath it from the outer room. A clatter of metal and the stoking of a fire soon confirmed that the woman of the house was up and about, and that a new day was dawning. Sitting on the edge of the bed and pulling on his boots, scraping a hand through his wayward, tousled brown hair, he stood and tentatively pulled back the curtain. The figure of a woman wrapped in a knitted shawl turned to face him, and gave him a piercing look as she appraised his appearance and demeanour.

"*Guten morgen* – good morning," he greeted her, at which she nodded and replied, "So ye're the sailor Jimmy brought home last night. I hope you are a clean living Christian man or ye'll not be welcome in this house."

Taking a moment to work out what she was saying, he nodded and assured her he was, and introduced himself as before.

"Good morning Robert. I'll be hoping ye slept well. Ye'll be welcome to a mug of tea and some porridge if you want. Sit down with ye," at which she indicated a chair by the table and going over to the rack produced a bowl and a china mug which she set down before him. Turning back to the stove, he could see that there was boiling pot she was in the process of stirring.

Footsteps from above heralded the arrival of Jimmy, who shouted, "Top o' the mornin' to ye Robert!" as he stomped down the stairs. "I see ye've met me good wife

Sarah. Mrs Geddis, this is Robert Kan … – Robert," eventually deciding to forgo trying to remember his surname.

"We've made our introductions, Jimmy. Now sit down and have yer porridge," she said briskly, while laying out spoons and pouring them both mugs of hot steaming tea from a pot boiling at the side of the stove.

Pleasantries over, she returned her attention to the porridge and soon they were all enjoying the steaming bowlfuls set before them. It was hot and filling, and that was the main thing, thought Robert. Then Sarah produced a loaf of bread and cutting thick slices, laid them on a board and set a dish of creamy butter alongside. The soda bread was a new experience for Robert and he found he enjoyed the sharp taste and the dense texture.

Having taken his fill of breakfast and the never ending cups of tea Sarah offered him, he asked Jimmy where he might find Mr Gilmore. Following his instructions, he walked back down to Shore Street, glancing to the left where a narrow steep lane ran up to a church, he assumed, as he could spy the steeple showing above the trees. Following the road down he could see the glint of the sun on the water of the harbour beyond. Between a row of houses were two larger dwellings, each of three storeys and having been told which one to look for, Robert arrived just as Mr Gilmore came out of the house, putting on his hat and buttoning up his coat.

"Aha, Kannenberg! Good morning. I hear you found accommodation with the Geddises. Good folk. Hope you had a good night's sleep and were well looked after?"

"Indeed," Robert assured him.

Falling into step beside him, Robert asked about the possibility of working for Gilmore again, as they strode down the hill towards the little harbour. For the next few years, Robert would become a regular crewman on his ships. But that was for the future. Today he was assured that there would be a need for him the following day – another trip to Scotland.

So he had a day to spend in Killyleagh. It was a fine day, with a brisk south-westerly breeze bringing the threat of rain later, but for the main part of the day it would remain clear. Robert returned to see Jimmy and Sarah Geddis and ask if it would be possible to have lodging for a while longer, to include all his meals while in port. An agreement was struck and Robert was soon to be a regular lodger in Back Street at their little house.

As he came out of their door, he turned and almost bumped into a young woman coming down the street. She gasped and nearly dropped the basket she was carrying, which was crammed with various vegetables. Clutching at the potatoes which had escaped, Robert stooped to pick them up and handing them to her with a smile, doffed his cap and begged her pardon.

"*Vergebungsbitte, Fräulein.*"

The girl looked at him with eyes wide and her brows raised, then frowned as she obviously didn't understand.

"I am sorry, miss," he tried again in his guttural Prussian accent.

"Oh!" she laughed, shaking back her dark hair.

"Let me help," he offered, indicating the overflowing basket.

"Sure, I'm only going to the house next door", she laughed. "I'm bringing my aunt some vegetables from the farm. But thank you."

Robert made a short sharp bow of his head, which caused her to laugh some more, and flicking back her long dark hair again, she opened the adjacent door and went inside. Robert had nothing else to do, so he walked back into the main shopping street of the town, that seemed to be called Front Street or High Street.

He hung about the street, whittling at a piece of wood with his knife as he perched on a water trough, while the people of the town went about their daily business. There seemed to be a fine variety of shops, no doubt well stocked from cargoes unloaded at the harbour. Some shops had windows displaying their goods, while some smaller ones traded from their front entrances. Outside were ranged racks stacked with various items, and hanging on rails above were a variety of hardware items for sale – pots, pans, tin baths, and so on. Taking a stroll the full length of the street, he noted at least half a dozen shops selling groceries of various types – some dairy based, some greengrocers, some dry goods. At least three shops boasted a variety of bonnets and hats, and there was also a selection of drapers stocking items for men and women. Shops selling oil lamps, china and earthenware complemented the collection, and he also noted a post office, a bootmaker, a baker and a butcher. And of course, at least three spirit and porter dealers. A bustling and busy little town indeed.

He headed up the gentle incline of the street to where it curved and found himself at the imposing entrance of, of all things, a castle. Not what he had expected to find – a *schloss*! There was a crenellated, stone-built entrance arch through which he could see the interior buildings. And to each side, stone towers with pointed roofs and narrow slit windows.

Turning right past the castle gates brought him to the top of Back Street, which would lead him down to the Geddis house again. Leaning against the wall of a workshop opposite, he lit a clay pipe he pulled from his pocket and enjoyed the sun on his face and the opportunity to think about the similarities to his home town of Ueckermünde, so very far away. He was roused from his reverie by a movement out of the corner of his eye, and was amused to see that the girl was just leaving the house next door to his lodgings.

If she noticed him hanging about outside, she made no acknowledgment as she left the house in the company of two young girls, and turned to head up the hill out of the village. Jumping up and crossing the road to fall in step with her, Robert doffed his black-peaked mariner's hat and made a showy bow, introducing himself and asking if he could walk with her. With a laugh, she remonstrated about what would people think – and her an unmarried girl! But there was a twinkle in her eye and he did not think that she really did worry about what anyone would think.

"I do not know your name, *Fräulein*. Please be so good as to tell me?"

"Ellen Magilton," she replied coquettishly. "And these are my two wee sisters, Mary and Frances."

"Pleased to meet you, Miss Ellen Majeelton," which was the best stab he could make at pronouncing her surname, "and Miss Mary and Miss Frances." At that the two little girls burst into fits of giggles and taking each other's hand, ran ahead of them up the street, while they followed walking in step up the hill, past the castle and out of the town.

It was about a mile to Shrigley, a tiny village north

of Killyleagh, a collection of cottages built to house the millworkers, a mill and a few outbuildings. The mill was beside a small river and Ellen explained it was a scutching mill, to turn the flax into fibres which would be made into the linen cloth. Robert got the gist of the description with gestures and some common words. Her father had a small-holding nearby as well as being the mechanic of the mill. And that is where the vegetables she had brought had been grown. As they neared her house, the two little girls had visibly slowed with the long walk, but now skipped ahead up the lane. Ellen said that perhaps he had better head back to Killyleagh now, but thanked him for his company, and turned and headed down the lane that led to a small whitewashed, two-storey house.

Turning on his heel, Robert headed back in the direction they had come, with a bounce in his step and humming a tune to himself.

CHAPTER FORTY

The following day dawned fine and with a moderate westerly breeze which would help them make good time on the crossing to Scotland. Sailing down the Lough and negotiating the tricky narrows between Portaferry and Strangford, they turned 'Friends' north east and her sails filled as they made for Ayrshire coast.

This was a route Robert got to know well over the next months, and he made the trip with a variety of cargoes, sometimes from Strangford to Girvan or Greenock, often finishing back at Strangford or Portaferry, but at other times continuing on the return journey up the coast a few more miles to Killyleagh, and when he did so, he would return to the Geddis house to lodge.

Gilmore had two other ships which Robert would sometimes see berthed beside them in one or other of the ports, and occasionally the crews would lay wagers on which of them would get home first. Braving some foul weather through the winter and spring gales, Robert was getting well used to crossing the Irish Sea, with only the occasional trip further south to Liverpool or the Isle of Man.

By the following year he was a regular visitor to Killyleagh, to Sarah and Jimmy's lodgings, and to the spirit dealers' back rooms that he would frequent on pay days. On more than one of these occasions, he would find himself on the end of taunts and jokes about being Prussian, or his broken English, and when he had downed a few glasses of porter or the local whiskey, he would often take on all-comers. It was not the first time he came back with Jimmy, arms around each other's shoulders propping each other up, to the house in Back Street, Robert nursing a black eye or a split lip. But he was usually the victor, so when Sarah berated him for turning up at her door like that, Jimmy would usually say, "Well ye should see the uther man!"

Robert was not a man to tangle with. He never lost his childhood short temper, and being stocky and strong he soon got a reputation but earned the respect of the local sailing crews as a good sailor, a hard worker and a reliable crew member.

With the Magilton family living next door, it was not surprising that Ellen and Robert often met – in the street, by the quayside or at church. Robert, although Evangelical by upbringing, found that the local parish church was a good enough match and he went there on the odd Sunday if he was in port and at a loose end. Never a very religious man, he made his own peace with God on the crest of a wave or in the eye of a storm, never feeling the need to be on his knees by his bedside or with his head bowed in church of a Sunday. But it was a good excuse to just happen to be there and catch Ellen's eye. He met the rest of her family, her father Hugh who worked as a mechanic at the scutching mill, his wife Margaret – a thin ascetic woman who always looked drawn and careworn, rarely raising a smile in his direction. Ellen had three younger brothers, James and Thomas, strapping lads of nineteen and fifteen, and Hugh aged twelve, then there was her sisters Eliza, a year younger than Thomas, and then Mary and Frances whom Robert had met that first day, and finally the baby of the family, Adelaide, barely four years old. After church the congregation would take their leave of the minister, and then form into groups where the chatter and laughter would ring out, while the latest gossip would be shared. Robert made a point of shaking Mr Magilton's hand when Ellen explained that Robert stayed with the Geddises on

Back Street. Hugh looked at Margaret and a knowing look passed between them.

CHAPTER FORTY-ONE

1872

As the following year turned from spring to summer, Robert found himself itching to get back to Killyleagh and walk up to Shrigley to see Ellen. And Ellen always felt a thrill when her Prussian sailor came calling. He was often invited to sit down for a meal in the kitchen and, sitting around the large scrubbed table, he would feel a small pang as it reminded him of similar times at home in Ueckermünde. The boys always liked to hear his tales of stormy voyages and as he became a natural storyteller, he found that his English was improving, though not his accent. Sometimes he would bring some fruit for the children, or tobacco that he had picked up on his travels, and he was doubly welcome then as Hugh stuffed his pipe and sat back by the fire, puffing contentedly, while Margaret and the girls cleared the table with a clattering of crockery and cutlery. After the boys had seen to the few livestock they kept – a pig and a cow, and Ellen came in from feeding the chickens and making the coop secure, he would share a glass with Hugh by the fireside and reluctantly admit to himself that he did miss a place to call home, as the thought of the trudge back to Killyleagh and a bed with Sarah and Jimmy would be his only reward.

He felt he could do a lot worse than Ellen. She was vivacious and a strong character, able to deflect his moods and flashes of temper with a laugh or a change of subject which inevitably had them both laughing together. And so after one such cosy evening, when everyone but Robert and Hugh had gone to their beds, Robert broached the subject of asking Hugh if he could take Ellen as his wife.

Hugh's face broke into a wide grin. "Sure, I thought ye'd never be gettin' round to it lad! If Ellen is willin' – and God knows I can't see why she wouldn't be," and here he winked at Robert, "then you may ask her outright and I'll give ye both my blessin'."

"*Danke*, thank you," replied Robert, with a sense of relief that he had got that over with. Smiling, he took one of the two proffered glasses from Hugh's hand and they clinked them together as Hugh announced "Here's tae ye both!"

When Robert returned to Killyleagh from Strangford at the beginning of the following week he walked the up the road to Shrigley and spotted Ellen collecting some peat from the stack by the door. Looking up, she gave him a wave, and wiping her hands on her apron, ran to the end of the lane to greet him. Giving her a hug and lifting her off her feet, he swung her round and thrilled at the tinkle of her laughter.

"Are you free to come for a walk just now?" he asked.

Nodding in reply, she ran inside and fetched a woollen knitted shawl which she wrapped around her, tucking the loose ends into the waistband of her skirt.

"I have to go into town to collect some things for Mammy but we can go together. Of course, we could go the long way round, through the fields ..." and here she looked sideways at him.

Smiling, they walked arm in arm through the gate that led into the green fields and away from the road. They talked about all sorts of things – inconsequential things, until Robert ran out of topics of conversation.

Falling silent, he took a deep breath and began, "I spoke

to your father last time I was here. He has given his – ach, what is the word ... ah, his permission, to allow me to offer you marriage. Will you become my wife Ellen?"

Ellen lifted her head and shook out her dark hair as she looked into the distance, leaving a silence between from them. Then she turned to him, feeling pity for him that she was playing this game and said, "Of course! I thought you'd never ask!" And at that she flung herself into his arms and they shared a long and enjoyable embrace.

CHAPTER FORTY-TWO

1872

As Robert could not be sure of his voyages and when he would be in Killyleagh, the couple hoped to marry in October and in the coming weeks, Ellen worked at collecting the things she would need for her new household. Together she and Robert made a list of what they would need, and between them and other members of the family they collected all the essentials. They had managed to rent a house in Breakey's Brae, which led off Back Street. It had one room downstairs and one above and was enough for them to start their new life together. While Robert was away at sea, Ellen worked at giving it a thorough clean and started to add the little touches which would make it home.

The next time Robert was in port, he went with Jimmy to buy a marriage licence and visit Reverend Moeran at the Parish Church. That way, he could marry Ellen, fitting in with his crewing commitments, and not have to wait three weeks for the Banns to be called. The minister knew the Magilton family well and had seen Robert in church on a few occasions. After talking with Robert for a short while, he was happy to issue the licence as both parties were residing in the Parish and satisfied his conditions.

For the first time in his life, Robert began to feel the tug of 'home' as he set sail the following week from Greenock and headed west across the truculent Irish Sea to his waiting bride. With only a day's notice, Ellen was both nervous and excited. She knew that they could not have a fixed date, but nevertheless she felt unprepared for what lay ahead when the day actually came – it was Saturday the nineteenth of October.

Ellen's younger brother Hugh had been sent to run into town the day before, once Robert had visited and informed them all that the wedding was set for the morrow. Calling in at his aunt and uncle's in Back Street, he gave them the news and they said they would round up the rest of the family who were able to attend. Then Hugh went to see his mother's brother, John Dick, who lived further up Back Street, also informing him of the wedding the following day.

Their wedding day dawned grey and drizzly, with a mist hanging over the water of the harbour and the masts of the ships at the quayside barely shadows looming though the hazy morning light. Robert was an early riser and, packing up his few belongings into his canvas bag, he prepared to enjoy his last hearty breakfast with Jimmy and Sarah before the events of the day would unfold.

Jimmy got him a sprig of 'lucky heather' to put in the buttonhole of the lapel of his jacket, and together they made their way down Back Street, over Cross Street and up Church Hill towards the spire of the church just visible through the mist.

Meanwhile Ellen was a jitter of nerves, her mother and sister were fussing round her and pinning up her thick hair and her brothers were getting the horse and cart ready to take them all into town. Eliza found a few wild flowers still growing in the hedgerows and tied them together with a blue ribbon, while her mother laid an Irish crocheted lace collar around the neckline of Ellen's best green dress; an heirloom from her mother, and then worn on her own wedding day twenty-five years earlier.

The cart trundled into town, coming round the bend of

the road in front of Killyleagh Castle and then down Back Street, continuing up Church Hill and through the entrance to the Church grounds. A few people were already walking quickly in the direction of the church doorway, pulling their mufflers close as the drizzle reached damp fingers into their collars. Ellen was grateful for the shawl over her head to keep off the worst of the dampness, but nevertheless she was glad to step down from the cart and head for the open door of the church and into the vestibule, shaking out her cloak and taking the posy handed to her by her sister Eliza. Turning to take her father's arm, she had those moments every bride experiences, wondering if this was what she wanted and if she was doing the right thing. But then she caught sight of Robert, as he turned around and looked up the main aisle of the church and caught her eye. With a hesitant smile, she took a deep breath and started forward. The congregation was not large. On the bride's side of the church were just a few friends and as many of the Magilton and Dick relatives as could be informed. Robert's side was even more sparse with only Sarah Geddis and a couple of mariner friends of Robert's. By Robert's side stood Jimmy Geddis, slicking down his hair and trying to look important.

As Ellen reached Robert's side and handed her posy to her sister to hold, she looked up at Robert, who, if she had but known it, was as nervous as she was. With no family of his own at his side, for the first time he truly felt their absence. The Reverend Moeran began the ceremony, "Dearly beloved, we are gathered here today in the sight of God ..."

It seemed to go by in a flash, and before she knew it, Ellen had a slim golden ring on her finger and had been soundly kissed by Robert as he was instructed by the minister, after pronouncing them man and wife. Taking the pen in his hand, Robert signed the register *Charles Robert*

Kannenberg in a strong hand, and then Ellen did so – *Ellen Margaret Magilton* for the last time, in a more deliberate and careful hand. Ellen asked Eliza to sign the register as a witness, at which she was thrilled, and John Dick, her uncle was the other signatory.

Lingering in the church vestibule, they received good wishes and congratulations from friends and family, before heading up into the town on the cart to the Dufferin Arms where they were to have their wedding meal. Mercifully the drizzle had lifted and as Robert glanced back towards the Lough, he could see the schooners' masts bobbing gently in the harbour. He had another trip in a couple of days, but for now he could enjoy being with Ellen and living as man and wife.

CHAPTER FORTY-THREE

1873/4

Robert was not a man who wrote letters or felt he had to keep in touch with family, but at Ellen's urging, he decided that he ought to write to his mother and tell her that he was now a married man. Putting it off for a few months, he eventually sat down and gathered together some paper, pens and ink and then deliberated about how to start the letter that he should have written years ago – he had been away from Ueckermünde for over ten years. In the end after sending her his greetings, he gave the basic facts about the intervening years, his marriage and where he now called home. Asking for some news from them in reply, he signed himself, "*Dein liebender Sohn, Robert.*" Ellen patted his shoulder and smiled at him, and then offered to walk with him to the Postal Office in the High Street where he could enquire about the postage to Prussia. How long it would take for a reply was questionable.

Ellen asked Robert to tell her about his family, and they would sit together by the fire of an evening while he told her what he knew about his father and grandfather, having never met either. He tried to describe the town of his birth and realised how similar it was to Killyleagh, the harbour, the bustling shops and businesses, the sailors who came and went – all so similar. Having never had his father at his side while he was growing up, he realised how much he wanted to be a father to his sons and help them make a life for themselves.

"It is time we had a family, Ellen," he announced one evening. Ellen smiled at him and silently hoped the same.

But many months went by, and every time Ellen's hopes were raised, they were to be dashed a few days later. After nearly a year and a half of marriage, there had been no sign of a pregnancy, and although Robert was often away for days at a time, there were plenty of times that they spent together when she had hoped that there would be a child this time.

Robert's temper had not lessened over the years, and he still got into arguments when he had had too much to drink after getting his pay. It was on one of these occasions when he met Ellen's father at Mary Milligan's public house at the far end of the town. Slapping him on the back, he bought Hugh a drink and together they sat enjoying a smoke and the company. But the conversation turned to family and marriage, and before long, Robert was bemoaning the fact that Ellen wasn't yet with child.

"In fact," he blustered, "I be thinking that I will be giving you your daughter back if she doesn't give me a son soon!"

Hugh shouted back at him, "Yer an uncouth bastard. How dare ye say such a thing about my darlin' Ellen. A good, God-fearing girl saddled with a boor of a man such as the likes of you! Mebbe it's not me darlin' girl that's the problem! Mebbe it's you, ya German scoundrel!"

A silence fell as heads turned and conversations stopped, shocked at what they had heard.

"Well, Mr Hugh Majeelton, let me tell you I *know* for a fact that it is not *my* problem! I have had no trouble in the past, that's certain! You can be sure of that!"

Hugh pushed back his chair with a scrape before it toppled behind him, and pulling himself up to his full height, suggested Robert came outside and repeated those words.

And that is what would have happened, had not a few of the customers got hold of the men's arms and kept them apart. Pushing Hugh back into a seat, they manhandled Robert to the door, where Mary loudly announced, "Get out of my place until ye can have a civil tongue in yer head!" and with that he was forcibly thrown into the road where he stumbled and almost found himself face down in the dirt.

Shouting back some choice phrases in German, he turned and headed down the road in the direction of the harbour, needing time to clear his head and defuse his temper. Sitting on a wooden pier overlooking the lapping grey water, he wondered what was wrong with his life and why Ellen was failing him. Eventually he turned up Shore Street and headed for home, and finding himself at his own door, felt the eyes of some of the neighbours on him, even though it was now nearly midnight. There wasn't a light on in the house, the fire was just a faint glow of the dying embers, and he couldn't bring himself to climb the stairs to face Ellen.

She found him slumped on a chair when she came down early the next morning to light the fire. By now Robert was ashamed at the words he had uttered in haste to her father, but he couldn't bring himself to tell her what had happened. Eating his breakfast in silence, he hoped he could patch up the rift between Hugh and himself, but wasn't sure how to go about it. Ellen got precious little out of him when she asked why he hadn't come up to bed last night, and in the end she gave up asking questions and went out with her basket to buy some provisions from the grocer in the High Street. Passing a few of her neighbours as she walked to the top of the Brae, she was aware of looks and whispered conversations. Women she knew refused to meet her gaze, and eyes were quickly averted as they turned to focus on something more important. Ellen felt distinctly uncomfortable.

Turning right into Back Street, and then walking up the hill with the castle towers visible through the gateway, she wondered what was wrong, what she had done to cause such looks. By the time she had turned left into the High Street which ran parallel to Back Street, she was more than a little perturbed. Would there be more looks and muttering behind her back? A few folk were about, carters loading and unloading at the shop doorways, the post being brought up from the harbour to be delivered to the Guiney's Post Office, sacks being shouldered from the coal cart, carcasses being delivered to Madine's the butcher, hides carried into Girven's the bootmaker, children racing up the hill to the National School, afraid of being punished for being late. Everything looked like just like normal. So why did she feel such apprehension?

As she went to open the door of Furey's the grocer, she almost walked into her cousin Catherine. Instead of stopping for a gossip as usual, Catherine gave a weak smile and made to walk past Ellen. Ellen decided that she needed to know what was going on.

"Catherine! Stop – where are you going? What's the matter?"

Catherine made to walk on, but then hesitated and turned to face her, her cheeks visibly reddening.

"Oh Ellen ...," she said, looking at her directly, but not knowing how to continue.

"What is it? For the love of God, tell me what is going on."

Coming closer and linking her arm through Ellen's, she turned them both to face down the street.

"Come with me, Ellen. We need to find somewhere we can talk. There are too many nosey folk around here," she added pointedly, looking at Mrs McGreevy who had altered course with the sole idea of getting near enough to hear what they were saying. With a sniff, the woman tossed her head, and walked past them with her nose in the air.

In the end they all but ran down the hill and up Church Hill Lane till they were in the peaceful solitude of the graveyard. Finding a flat stone to sit on, "Beggin' yer pardon Mr Patterson," Catherine quipped, she took Ellen's hand in hers. Not knowing how to begin she looked earnestly at Ellen, whose brown eyes were boring into her green ones.

"Tell me, Catherine – or I shall burst! Sure, is it something I've done? I just don't know!"

"Well ..., oh Ellen, it's all around the town. Bertie came in last night from Ma Milligan's and woke me up to tell me what happened. Seems yer Pa and Robert had words, and then Robert said he was for givin' ye back to yer Pa 'cos ye couldn't give him a bairn, an' then ..." – and here she took a deep breath, as Ellen's face started to crumple, "... and he said he knew it weren't his fault as he'd no trouble in the past! Oh Ellen! ..."

Covering her face in her hands, Ellen doubled over and sobbed at the hurt and shame that she felt at Robert's words. What did he mean? Did he mean what everyone obviously thought he meant? How could she face him? How could she face anyone?

"Of course, all the men that were there last night came home and – well, ye knows how quickly gossip spreads in this place ..." Pausing to put her arms around Ellen and stroke her hair, while her body heaved with sobs, she spent the next half hour calming her and mopping her tears.

"What will ye do?" she asked.

Taking a deep breath, Ellen said tremulously, "I have to speak to Robert. He'll have said too much – it's that temper of his. He won't have meant it I'm sure."

Catherine gave her a look that indicated that she wasn't so sure, but supporting her cousin to stand, and smoothing down their skirts and tightening their shawls around them, they started walking slowly out of the churchyard and in the direction of home. Ellen told Catherine she didn't want her coming in, even though Catherine was all for tackling Robert herself. This was between her and Robert. She wanted to hear what he had to say for himself.

Closing the door behind her, she was partly relieved and partly taken aback to find Robert virtually where she had left him, sitting at the table with his head in his hands. She had wanted time to plan what she would say, but now she had to face him without being able to rehearse her words. At first he didn't look up or acknowledge her entrance, but then he slowly lifted his head and looked in her direction, immediately registering her puffy eyes and blotchy cheeks.

"Ellen ..." he began, but she cut him off as she raised both hands as if to fend off his excuses.

"How could you? How could you!" she said, her voice rising with emotion.

"I did not mean to, it's not what you think."

"Well maybe you had better explain to me what you

did mean!" she snapped back, her voice rising even further.

Robert stood and took a step towards her, at which she took a step backwards. "Please Ellen, let me explain." He realised that she did not necessarily know what had been said, but obviously she had heard something, and that was enough to have upset her badly.

Taking two more steps towards her, he took her hands in his and drew her closer to him. "Ellen, I would do nothing to hurt you or upset you, you know that. I should not have had so much of that whiskey – your father certainly enjoys his drink."

"From what I have heard, it is not what my father said that is the problem," Ellen replied curtly, trying to release her hands, but Robert held them firm.

"I love you with all my heart Ellen. I dream of the day when we will have a family of our own. It is my earnest wish," at which his face crumpled seeing the hurt he had caused her.

"You know that is what I want most in the world too, Robert, with you at my side. But from what I hear, you might have a family somewhere already!"

Robert gasped, "No Ellen! No! That was just my temper and the words I spoke were just to throw at your father. I swear! Please believe me, you are the only woman for me – and you always have been."

Pulling her closer, he closed his arms around her and kissed her tears away.

"Oh Robert. I love you so, but you can be so hurtful. The things you say and do. Your temper will ruin you if you are not careful."

"I know, I know, *liebling*," he whispered. 'I am so sorry. Please forgive me." And he continued kissing her until her tears stopped and he felt her relax in his arms.

CHAPTER FORTY-FOUR

1874/5

It took more time to bring Hugh Magilton round, and it was painfully hard for Robert to have to face him and beg his forgiveness for the words he had uttered. But time heals, and after a few months the cruel words were, if not forgotten, then at least put in the past.

Robert continued making trips back and forth across the Irish Sea for Joseph Gilmore in one or other of his ships, 'Iona' or 'Friends', and became a well-respected mariner, so much so that Gilmore said it was about time Robert should think about taking his Mates Certificate. Then he would be in charge of a crew of his own on the voyages, and he could also pay him more. Gilmore saw in him the makings of a skilled seaman and, on more than one occasion, his skill had been noted by other ships' masters as well. He needed a character testimonial from a Master or Ship-owner, which Gilmore was willing to provide; in the end it would be mutually beneficial as Gilmore would have a man he could trust at the helm of one of his ships, and Kannenberg would be progressing his career.

Robert asked about what it would require in the way of examinations, English not being his first language, but Gilmore gave him a booklet to look at, which outlined what he would need to be able to do in the five hour examination, which would be held in Belfast.

Robert thanked Gilmore and that evening sat with Ellen looking over the requirements as outlined in the booklet Gilmore had given him. It seemed to demand a lot from what Robert could see, and he knew he was not a natural scholar, though he did think he was a natural mariner.

Ellen and he read through it aloud together ...

The entrant must write a legible hand and understand the first five rules of arithmetic, and the use of logarithms. He must be able to work a day's work complete, including bearings and distance of the port he is bound to, by Mercator's method; to correct the sun's declination for longitude, and find his latitude by meridian altitude of the sun; and to work such other easy problems of a like nature as may be put to him. He must understand the use of the sextant, and be able to observe with it, and read off the arc.

He must also be able to observe and calculate the amplitude of the sun, and deduce the variation of the compass therefrom, and be able to find the longitude by chronometer by the usual methods. He must know how to lay off the place of the ship on the chart, both by bearings of known objects, and by latitude and longitude. He must be able to determine the error of a sextant, and to adjust it, also to find the time of high water from the known time at full and change.

IN SEAMANSHIP – He must give satisfactory answers as to the rigging and unrigging of ships, stowing of holds, & so on; must understand the measurement of the log-line, glass, and lead-line; be conversant with the rule of the road, as regards both steamers and sailing-vessels, and the lights and fog signals carried by them, and will also be examined as to this acquaintance, with 'the Commercial Code of Signals for the use of all Nations.'

He must also know how to moor and unmoor, and to keep a clear anchor; to carry out an anchor; to stow a hold; and to make the requisite entries in the ship's log. He will also be questioned as to his knowledge of the use and management of the mortar and rocket lines in the case of the stranding of a vessel, as explained in the official log-book.

The candidates will be allowed to work out the various

problems according to the method and the table they have been accustomed to use, and will be allowed five hours to perform the work; at the expiration of which time, if they have not finished, they will be declared to have failed, unless the Local Marine Board see fit to extend the time.

To be honest, Ellen didn't understand half of what was in the document, but actually Robert did when they read it out together. Even he was pleasantly surprised to realise how much he had learned over the last ten or more years. As for the practicalities, he could look over some of the manuals which were available, and they could get the required fee of 10 shillings together. He would have to ride up to Belfast and stay over for a night, as the examination would be scheduled for the next morning. If he left straight away after it finished, he should be back in Killyleagh that night.

Over the next few weeks Robert put in more studying than he felt he had ever done, and in between voyages he would make sure he gave Ellen plenty of his time as he never forgot those unkind words and thoughtless actions of the past.

The date for the examination was set for early August 1874 and when Robert returned from Belfast, he was mentally as well as physically exhausted. However Ellen wanted to know all about it; how did he get on, was it as hard as he'd thought, how did he think he had done, when would he know if he had passed? And what was Belfast like? What were the ladies dressed like? And ... Robert stopped her in her tracks and with a laugh said he would tell her all about it but, "Woman I need a cup of tea!" At least, thought Ellen to herself, he was having less of the drink these days and that could only be a good thing.

About a week later, the postal delivery boy came by late one afternoon with an official-looking letter for Mr

C R Kannenberg. Taking it from him with shaking hands, Ellen laid it down in the centre of the table, where it would await Robert's return from his trip from Greenock tomorrow.

Together they opened it and Robert proudly showed her the cream coloured paper covered in flowing lettering which stated that: *'The Lords of the Committee of Privy Council for Trade have granted a Certificate of Competency as Only Mate to Robert Kannenberg, this eighth day of August 1874. Signed Thomas Gray, one of the Secretaries to the Board of Trade.'*

Taking Ellen in his arms, he lifted off her feet and swung her round and round, both whooping in delight as he did so. Falling dizzy and exhilarated onto the rug in front of the black-leaded range, they hugged each other and planned for a better, more secure future.

CHAPTER FORTY-FIVE

1845 - 1847

Gilmore was delighted that Robert had his Mates Certificate and gave him charge of the 'Friends' as the previous mate was now getting older and had decided it was time to give up going to sea, having fallen on the last trip and badly damaged his knee. Robert took charge of the loading and unloading of cargoes as diverse as beans, coal and timber and sailed across the capricious Irish Sea, facing up to the challenges of weather she threw at him, and beating her every time. He became known as a man who would take a ship out when others wouldn't, and that he would get the most out of a ship to bring her to port in the best possible time. With a crew of three other men, they became regulars in Girvan, Liverpool, and Greenock. 'Friends' was a sound ship, and Robert loved when her sails billowed out in a strong wind from her two stout masts, and they ploughed headfirst through the rolling waves, spray flying and leaving a churning wake behind them, with only the seabirds for company and the shriek of the wind.

Coming back into port one cold late February night, he saw Ellen was there to meet him, her shawl over her head and her coat buckled tight around her. Together they walked homeward and gratefully opened the door to their cosy little house up the Brae, happy to close out the wind and holding out their hands to the stove for warmth. Later that evening, as they talked about inconsequential matters and the local gossip, Ellen grew serious and looked Robert in the eye.

"Robert, there is something I must tell you ..." at which

Robert's smile faded and he sat forward in his chair. "What you have always wanted has happened. You are going to be a father."

It took a few seconds for Robert to process the news, then he went to her and swept her into his arms. With tears glistening in his eyes, he kissed her gently and then asked, "When will this be?"

"September I think."

"Are you alright? Sit down."

"I'm fine," she laughed. "I feel just fine. Everything is going to be just perfect."

On the twelfth of September, after a trouble-free pregnancy, Ellen went into labour and, with her mother by her side, gave birth to healthy girl whom they named Margaret Henriette Louise. Margaret, after Ellen's mother, and Henriette after Robert's mother. She was baptised in the Parish Church where Robert and Ellen had married four years previously. Robert strode around the town so proudly, feeling that he had vindicated all the gossip and finally put to bed the idea that he was not man enough to be a father. Her Magilton grandparents doted on the child and everyone agreed she was the image of her mother. But Robert could see some of his own mother in her, wishing that she was here to see her latest granddaughter.

And so he sat down to think about composing another letter to his mother. The last one he had written was over four years ago, telling her of his marriage to Ellen. It had taken many months to receive any reply, but when he did it was evident why that was the case. His oldest sister, Marie, by then in her mid-thirties, had married a widower in Berlin and, as she was the last of the children and had been living with his mother in Ueckermünde, the decision was made to have her mother living with them in Berlin. So the letter that he had sent, arriving in Ueckermünde, had then to be redirected after an address had been found for Frau Kannenberg. And by the time the letter had found its way to her, Marie had been delivered of a stillborn child. So the reply that he eventually received from his mother took nearly a year to arrive, giving him news of his siblings and their growing families, but also of those who had passed as well – both young and old. She admitted that she herself was feeling her age, and missed her friends in Ueckermünde, but was glad to be near her children and grandchildren in Berlin.

So Robert was motivated to update her on her newest granddaughter, little Louise who, thanks be to God, was thriving and was the very apple of his eye. He also told her about his promotion, having gained his Mates Certificate, and the hope that soon, they would be able to move to a larger house in Killyleagh.

Walking to the postal office in Back Street on a stormy January day, he looked out at the harbour and the masts of the ships being thrown this way and that in a mad dance. The wind was whipping the spray off the tops of the waves that blew onshore and he knew that further out of the shelter of the harbour, the Irish Sea would be a maelstrom as the south westerly wind funnelled up between Ireland and Scotland. He was due to sail later that day, and so it was for that reason that, after posting the letter which he doubted would make the packet from Belfast on the morrow, he stood by the quayside, clamping his peaked cap tightly onto his head, while scanning the sky and the sea for clues of any break in the weather. He was due to take 'Friends' to Strangford, then pick up a cargo bound for Girvan.

Striding back home, he considered the options. Waiting for better weather would cost Gilmore money, as the cargo would be delayed arriving at the Ayrshire port. But running before a storm, although something which always gave him a thrill, was also foolhardy if he was to risk the crew or the ship.

Banging the door behind him to keep out the screaming fingers of the icy wind, he took in the cosy domestic scene in front of him. Ellen was stirring a pot on the top of the black-leaded stove and the enticing smell of fresh bread emanated from the small oven beneath. Baby Louise was in her small crib in the corner making tiny gurgling and cooing sounds, obviously having just been fed and changed and now feeling content. It was a moment to cherish and one he never wanted to risk again.

The next morning the wind appeared to have abated somewhat and so, after assembling the crew and checking the cargo of potatoes, oats and butter, Robert took 'Friends' out of the small harbour and navigating through the choppy waters of the lough, made his way to Strangford. But there the wind was coming full force up the channel of the Irish Sea and beyond the shelter of Strangford, it looked ferocious. Many ships crowded the port of Strangford and, across the narrow stretch of water, its opposite number Portaferry. Lashed together in ranks, they were all awaiting better weather. Some looked the worse for wear, having just made it to port the previous night, some with damaged sails and one with a splintered mast. Gilmore had to agree that it would be foolhardy to risk taking any ship out in this weather and that they would delay leaving port until tomorrow.

That day dawned a degree calmer, and although some masters were not of a mind to chance the crossing, Robert wanted to give it a go, anxious to complete the job and return home as soon as possible. By now he was getting a reputation as a mariner who would take on the winds and the weather – some might have called him reckless, but others would nod their heads with respect and call him skilled. The crossing was not an easy one, but using all the skills he had acquired over the years, and by giving clear and competent orders to the three-man crew, they nosed into port in Girvan and tied up at the harbour to unload their cargo.

By the next day the storm had blown itself out and there was even a weak sun spilling rays from the gaps in the clouds, which were slowly parting to herald a fine day. They made good time on the return journey and it was pleasant sailing all the way, although bitterly cold in the clear air. Standing behind the wheel, and watching the sails, ready to give orders to trim or stow them, to prepare to tack or to heave to, Robert was in his element. The sea was dotted with other vessels making the crossing east-west and others north-south. What was more noticeable in the last few years were the number of steam ships that now plied these waters. With both sail and steam engines to propel them, they were less at the mercy of the winds, being more manoeuvrable, and were both faster and better able to carry heavier cargoes. Robert wondered whether that was the future for cargo vessels, and whether he might have to adapt and learn a new skill. Already Gilmore was casting an eye at the competition and hinting that adding a steam vessel or two to his fleet might enable him to steal a march on his rivals. Steam was the future; sail was the past.

CHAPTER FORTY-SIX

1877

Their lives moved to the rhythm of the winds and tides. When the weather was fair, Robert would be away on various trips and when the winds dropped altogether or screamed in protest, Robert would be in a distant port or at home with his little family in Killyleagh. If she was honest, and listened to the little voice that crept in to niggle her at quiet moments, Ellen worried when Robert was away and although she loved her brave sailorman, she also feared for his safety and stood waiting anxiously with the other wives for his arrival at the mouth of the harbour when the claws of the blustery winds threatened to reach out and snatch at the little ships.

By autumn of that year, Louise was toddling around and into everything. Naturally everything she picked up went into her mouth, and Ellen had to keep her eyes on her every minute. She was always hungry, and now onto mashed solids which Ellen prepared so that they could all sit down together at a family mealtime. Ellen was now no longer feeding her herself and was soon able to confirm that she was pregnant again. Robert was delighted, but realised that before long they would need to start thinking about the future. They would soon be outgrowing their little two-roomed house.

Taking on as many jobs as he could, Robert worked hard at getting some money put away. He opened a savings account at the Post Office in the High Street, and Mr Guiney was pleased to see that Kannenberg was at last, putting down roots and facing up to his responsibilities.

In fact it became almost an obsession with Robert. He would try to put something into his account every week or two and nothing gave him more pleasure than to see the totals in the columns growing each time.

It was nearly Christmas and a spattering of sleet and snow lay on the rooftops of Killyleagh. The sky was leaden and the town seemed to feel as if it were being pressed down by the oppressive sky and glowering clouds. No-one stayed out any longer than necessary and lights shone in windows all day to illuminate the gloomy interiors. Robert was due to return from Girvan tomorrow, and Ellen tried to quell her unease which she always felt when he was away. Resting her hands on the curve of her gently swelling belly, she pulled back the thin curtain from the window and looked out at the alleyway outside the house. Hardly a soul was about, and when anyone passed it was only a quick tapping of their boots that broke the silence, as they made for the warmth of their fire. Hoisting Louise on her hip, and wrapping her thick knitted shawl around them both, she hooked her other arm through her basket and shut the door quickly behind her to preserve the heat in the room. The outing was as short a one as she could make, and once she had bought flour and butter from Furey's the grocer and had quickly gone next door to buy a reel of cotton from Mary Field's drapery shop, she rewrapped them both together and headed homeward down the street. As always, she lifted her eyes to the harbour in the distance, wondering where Robert was and if he would be safely home by the next day, Christmas Eve. There was an eerie stillness and yet the leaden clouds seemed to be building in the distance. Crooning to Louise, who had started to whimper with the cold on her cheeks, she snuggled her up and turned up Back Street and into Breakey's Brae. A neighbour nodded in passing with a quick comment about the bitter weather, but neither of them had any inclination to stop and chat.

Closing the door behind her, and feeling the welcoming warmth of the room, she slid Louise down onto the floor and said, "Daddy will be home tomorrow, me darlin'. Won't that be nice?"

To which Louise chanted, "Dada, Dada!" with a toothy smile, as a dribble ran down her chin.

Ellen woke during the night to the sound of a crash as something was blown over outside. It was followed by more rattling and rumbling and sounded like a metal bucket bowling down the alley in the increasing wind. It shrieked through the gaps in the window frame and rattled at the loose fitting door. Louise started to cry, having been woken, and Ellen pulled her closer to her and wrapped the blankets around them both, while rocking her to sleep with soothing words and promises of Daddy coming home tomorrow.

Meanwhile Robert was preparing to set sail from Girvan in the teeth of the gale, his mind fixed on getting home to celebrate Christmas with his little family and bringing with him a little doll for Louise and a paisley shawl for Ellen. These he had wrapped in oilcloth and stowed beside his canvas bag in the locker below deck. A north-westerly wind would help him head south-east, in order to make port at Strangford before daylight faded. Robert knew the waters, knew the rocks, knew the sandbars and the vagaries of the currents like the back of his hand, and this morning nothing was going to stop him from setting out for home. The three crew were his regulars – Patrick, a man of about his own age, Joseph, older, with years of being a fisherman with his own boat, but now resigned to sailing for another master, and Willie the youngest at nineteen, who reminded Robert of himself at that age – ready to take on the world. But they were together in a huddle by the mooring rope when he looked over, ready to give them the order to get underway. Eventually Patrick broke away from the group and came towards him, his oil-skin flapping in the wind.

"Are ye sure ye want to be sailin' in this? It's awfy fierce, sure 'tis, an' looks like it's only set to get worse."

"You want to be home, don't you? We can make it. We've warm homes and good women waiting for us. We've been out in worse than this before. Have you checked the coal is well stowed? Then we'll cast off and let's make for home, Paddy."

And with that, he pulled the black shiny peak of his cap further down over his eyes and gave the order.

Afterwards, the reports of that day in the newspapers gave the wind as a force eleven gale, which caused many a ship's crew to forego their Christmas in the comfort of their home port. But it also reported ships that had foundered and crews' lives that had been lost.

Fighting their way through the wind and waves every inch of the way, and being thrown around like a cork, the little schooner buried her bows in the troughs of the waves and then pitched back up, shedding water over the deck and through the scuppers. Robert's skill and expertise were tested to the utmost, and they were soon nearing the end of the thirteen mile crossing of the North Channel, and were in sight of the Ards peninsula, the strip of land that marked the eastern side of Strangford Lough. The lights of Cloughey, and Kearney beyond, could be seen in the fading light and between them, the new lightship marking the South Rock appeared and disappeared over the crests of the waves. The South Rock itself barely protruded above the water, and was a graveyard for many a ship that didn't give it due deference and a wide berth. On it stood the stout round granite tower of the wave-swept Kilwarlin Light, although now the new lightship had been commissioned to replace it. In that grey squally dusk, neither were easily seen and it was pure dead-reckoning that Robert had to rely on.

Feeling the wrench and tug of the wind as it toyed with them that afternoon, Robert's knuckles showed white and his arms ached as his muscles strained with the effort of maintaining the course he had set. One minute he could see the light to his starboard and then next, it loomed in front of him as they were spiralled round and the sea drove them straight on, onto the edge of the rocks. The shock of the impact, followed by the chilling sound of splintering wood, soon confirmed that they were indeed victims of the notorious hazard to shipping. The waves dragged them off, then drove them forward again before they were impaled on the rocks for a second time. The cargo of coal, although in sub-divided sections, had started to shift and tumble to lie on the starboard side of the hold.

Catching sight of Willie huddled in the lee of the deckhouse, his eyes like saucers, spurred Robert into action. Glancing at the light ship, he caught intermittent signals from the men on deck as they swung a lantern and tried to shout to them over the waves, waving and gesticulating at them.

Robert caught disjointed phrases ... "coastguard ... stay on board ... hang on ...," from which he eventually deduced that the lightship had signalled for the Cloughey coastguard and that a boat had been launched. Leaving the 'Friends' would be the last resort and they should stay on board as long as they possibly could, for once in the water, they would have no chance; they would be swept away and lost in an instant.

Realising that there was no way that they could wrench themselves free of the rocks, Robert cupped his hands around his mouth to shout, "Lash yourself to anything solid. We have to stay on board as long as possible. A boat is coming!" And just as he did so, a huge wave broke over the port side and his feet were taken from under him, sweeping him against the rail of the ship which was now at a sickening angle.

It seemed an age before a light was seen bobbing between the troughs of the waves, and it was with relief that Robert saw a line of men rowing towards them for all they were worth. They were tossed and battered by the waves but managed to put themselves between the lightship and the 'Friends'. Robert cupped his hands around his mouth and gave the order, "Abandon ship!" Using a rope that the men on the coastguard skiff had thrown to them, Patrick and Joseph made their way through the surging waves towards the strong arms of the coastguard crew, bulky in their cork lifejackets, who dragged them unceremoniously into the narrow boat. Hauling at Willie, who was plainly terrified, Robert dragged him over the rail, having attached a line to him, and then watched as the lad half swam, half dragged himself over to the skiff, where pairs of hands hauled him up over the side.

Now there was only Robert left aboard. Time stood still while he considered his options. Stay with the ship, or abandon her to her fate and make for the rescue boat. Seconds seemed to stretch out interminably while he weighed up his chances. His loyalties to Gilmore were plain – and he would want to save the ship if he could. She was an old and faithful friend who had seen him through many a storm and been his faithful protector through them all. She had never wavered in her loyalty to her crew nor put their lives at risk, she had been windproof and watertight, home and comfort through all their years together. He just couldn't abandon her to her fate. If he could take shelter in the wheelhouse and weather the storm, he could get the coastguard to send a message to Gilmore and get a squad out to refloat her and bring her home to port at the first break in the weather. As this option seemed to be the one he would choose, a massive wave broke over her, and as she was thrown onto her side, the hideous splintering of wood made him turn to see one of her masts falling amid a tangle of rigging and sailcloth. At that, another creak and groan and water came gushing through her hull, as she broke her back upon the rocks. It was the final death knell for his faithful friend. As he looked around, grabbing the log books, papers, anything he thought he ought to bring with him, he went below and sought out his packages wrapped in oilcloth. Grabbing his canvas bag and undoing the slip knots as best as he could, with fingers wet and numb with cold, he stuffed the papers next to the presents for Louise and Ellen, and as he did so, he suddenly knew exactly what he had to do. He had to save himself and get back for them. They were his responsibility, above that of the ship.

Appearing again above deck, he could make out the faint shouts snatched away by the wind, urging him to leave her now. The faint swinging of a light helped him pinpoint the rescue boat's direction, as the salt spray lashed his face and blurred his vision. Knowing every inch of the ship as if she was his other mistress, he felt his way to the rail, sliding over the deck as it sloped towards the sea and the rocks. Grasping for the rope that had been tied off as a guideline, he threw his legs over the rail and landed amidst surging freezing water and jagged slippery rocks. Hanging onto the rope, he hauled his way along it until he felt hands grabbing at his jacket and he was pulled into the safety of the skiff, which was battling to keep its position and clear of the voracious rocks.

Collapsing in a heap, he bent his head and whispered, "*Leb wohl, mein lieber alter Freund.* Farewell, my dear old friend."

◆ ◆ ◆

In the early hours of the twenty-fourth of December, the coastguard boat brought three shocked and shivering seaman to Cloughey quayside. With them, sitting upright and wrapped in an oilskin, was another man, with his black peaked cap still firmly on his head and his back straight as he looked directly ahead. What was he feeling? Relief, regret, shame, dishonour?

Within the hour a telegraph message had been sent to Portaferry for the attention of Mr Joseph Gilmore. "*Schooner 'Friends' lost South Rock. Crew saved.*" A messenger was sent to ride to Killyleagh and arrived there in the afternoon.

Ellen had been tidying up and arranging a few holly boughs over the mantel as a seasonal welcome for Robert when he came home. She was concerned at the weather, and although the winds had eventually abated, it was still gusty and she was unsure if he would have sailed in last night's weather. She thought better of walking down to the quayside with baby Louise to await his arrival, knowing he would be striding up the hill as soon as he could, and there was no need for them both to be stood out in the cold.

The light was fading that late winter afternoon when Ellen heard footsteps approach, then stop outside her step, followed by a knock at the door. Robert wouldn't knock. Who could be calling on such a wild winter's day?

Tentatively opening the door, she was met with the ashen face of Patrick McArdle's wife. Ushering her in out of the cold, she searched her eyes for the reason of her visit.

"Oh Mrs Kannenberg – the message has just come from Portaferry. The rider came just a wee while ago. The ship's gone down."

Ellen's hand shot to her mouth to stifle the gasp that tried to escape. Her legs turned to water and she reached for the nearest chair.

"Dear God," she whispered. "The men?"

"I've been told they're safe but I don't know the details. But I thought I should let you know, you'll have been waitin' and wonderin' no doubt."

"Thank God they're safe. D'ye think they'll be home soon?"

"I don't know m'dear but like you, I've a wee brood at home waiting for their Da. Have ye anyone to wait wi' ye?"

"I'll be fine. I'd rather wait for Robert here with Louise. Thank you for letting me know." And she reached out her arms to her for a moment's embrace, to share their matching emotions of fear and relief.

After closing the door behind her, Ellen crumpled onto the chair by the fire and covered her face in her apron, allowing her sobs full rein. Stifling them so as not to wake the sleeping Louise, she began rocking backwards and forwards to try to give herself some release. Eventually her sobs subsided and she turned to look at little Louise, mercifully still sleeping on their bed, snuggled under a pile of blankets.

"Daddy won't be home today," she whispered, leaning over the child and brushing a stray lock of fine hair from her face.

The men were brought over from Cloughey by cart the next morning, Christmas Day. Mr Gilmore was told of their imminent arrival and arranged to meet them in the back room of the Dufferin Arms. After expressing his relief that they were all safe, the other men were allowed to get home to their families. Looking sternly at Robert, he demanded to know the full story. So Robert explained that all had been well until a rogue wave had caught them and spun them round, causing them to be driven onto South Rock.

"Why the devil didn't you wait out the storm and shelter at Girvan? I've heard many did, including one of my other ships. Why in God's name did you risk my ship and my cargo? Foolishness? Bravado?" And at that he shook his head a let out a great gasp of exasperation. "I thought you were a better sailor than that. You should have known better – and look what has been the result."

And with that, he turned his back and walked from the room, leaving Robert feeling angry and confused in equal measure. If he had made it to port safely, Gilmore would have been shaking his hand and praising his skill, slapping him on the back and congratulating him for his prowess in bringing his cargo safely to port. Robert had never lost a ship. He knew what he was doing better than most, if not all, the men in those parts. He had a good reputation and yet Gilmore had just stripped him of all his pride and made him feel like a child. His cheeks reddened and his hands clenched and unclenched at his side. Turning to the door, he punched out and slammed his fist into the door frame, venting his fury and releasing all the pent up emotion of the last thirty-six hours.

Turning into the saloon bar, he ordered a whiskey and shot it back in one go, then demanded another. He was physically shaking and leaning his elbow on the worn wood of the counter, rested his chin on it and closed his eyes. He took several deep breaths before he opened his eyes again, looking at himself in the mirror behind the bar, framed by shelves of bottles and glasses. And laid across the top of the mirror were several boughs of holly and evergreen branches. Slowly realisation came upon him. It was Christmas Day. This is not where he should be.

Pushing back the stool, he threw a few coins on the bar beside the unfinished whiskey, and headed for the door – and home.

CHAPTER FORTY-SEVEN

1877 - 1878

Amidst all the uncertainty at the start of the new year, Fate seemed to take a hand. Gilmore was, naturally, wary of entrusting another ship to Robert's hand, nor did he have a vacancy for a mate, as all his other ships were fully crewed. But Robert had to provide for his growing family. He made trips for the odd master needing a short local voyage to deliver goods, or filled in at the last minute when a ship was a crewman short, but there was no long-term work in prospect and no local ship owner was willing to give him regular work.

It was Hugh, Ellen's father, who was instrumental in steering the little family on their new course. He heard that a house at the top of Clay Road had fallen vacant, in the tiny hamlet of Toye, which merely consisted of the house, a blacksmith, a few outbuildings and a couple of neighbouring cottages. It was in need of some tidying up but Ellen wasn't shy of a bit of hard work, and together they strode out on a cold but bright February morning to walk the couple of miles to Toye. Of course, Louise had to come too and loved nothing better than to be on her father's shoulders, straining to see over the hedgerows, bundled up in coat, shawl, mittens and woolly hat. As they strode along, their breath making clouds around them, Robert noticed how many smallholdings they passed. Some were merely a cottage with a scrap of land attached, others were more substantial, but all were fairly isolated, being amongst fields and countryside, now desolate and rimed with frost, twinkling as the low sun peered weakly though the bare branches of the trees that bordered each side of the country road. But the road they walked was the main road which connected Killyleagh with Comber and onwards, to eventually reach Belfast.

On reaching the house, Robert took in the neighbouring smithy and adjacent low cottages that lay along one side of the V-shaped junction. The house lay along the other side of the V and had a few ramshackle outbuildings in a yard. It was a single storey but brick built and with a slate roof, which looked in reasonably good condition. From the point of the V in the road, they faced the end of the house which had two chimneys – one at each gable. The front door was in the centre of the front of the house, flanked by a window on each side.

They had been given the key by the local land agent, as they would be leasing the property, and so, as it turned reluctantly in the lock of the worn wooden door, they were able to walk inside. There was a small entrance hallway with stone flags which opened left and right into a room each side. To the left was the kitchen with a black-leaded range, that needed a bit of elbow grease, thought Ellen, and to the right another large room with a fireplace. On either side of the flagged passage beyond, another pair of doors opened left and right into two smaller rooms. At the opposite end of the hallway from where they had entered, a door at the far end opened out into the yard and to the right was the attached outbuilding, presently used a store for all manner of clutter.

Ellen loved the house immediately and was already planning what she could do to clean and brighten it up. Robert also was appraising the possibilities that lay in the house as, while they had been walking there, a plan had begun to form itself in his mind.

On the return journey, Louise wanted to walk and toddled along ahead of them for a while before falling over and starting to cry. Scooping her up in his arms, Robert hoisted her onto his shoulders again as she whooped with laughter, her tears forgotten. Soon she was nodding, resting the side of her head on his cap, and for the rest of the journey they heard not a peep from her.

The baby was due in May and they both hoped that they would be settled in Toye in time for the birth. And so it was, that they moved their meagre belongings one drizzly morning in April, piled up on a hired cart with Louise sitting on Ellen's lap, while Robert took the reins and headed out of Breakey's Brae, down to Cross Street and headed out along the Comber road bound for Toye.

Although Ellen was now feeling large and awkward, conversely she felt energised and keen to get the house feeling like home. Coming out with Robert on a few occasions had allowed her to get the major part of the cleaning done. A good sweeping out, followed by mopping the flagstone passage and kitchen. Then, black-leading the range and clearing out the fireplaces. And finally hanging some curtains she had put together from some material she had pleaded Robert to buy at Cleland's in the High Street.

As soon as they arrived in Toye, Robert set Louise down to explore the house, while helping Ellen clamber awkwardly from the cart. The first job she set to was getting a fire lit in each of the fireplaces, and lighting the stove and getting a kettle of water on to boil. Robert untied and unloaded their belongings from the cart – the bed frame and mattress, a couple of chairs, a table, a trunk with linens and clothing, sundry crockery and kitchen utensils, a thin rug and a tin tub and washboard. Leading the horse round into the yard, he tied him up and fed him some oats, while stroking his flank.

Soon there was a shout from Ellen to come and get some tea, followed by Louise running into the yard shouting for her Dada! Swinging her into his arms, he strode in through the back door and set her down as she ran off to explore every room, over and over again, the novelty of having so much space to stretch her pudgy little legs making her laugh and scream with delight.

◆ ◆ ◆

Ellen went into labour in the third week of May and Robert fetched her mother Margaret on the cart. Keeping Louise occupied picking wildflowers in the small adjoining bit of field, he could still hear Ellen's groans coming from the house. But then all was quiet and he and Louise ventured back as Margaret came to the back door, smiling.

Leaving Louise with her grandmother, he went into the bedroom where the sun was streaming in and lighting up the scene before him. Ellen was sitting up in bed, strands of her brown hair escaping from her thick braid and sticking to her damp forehead. In her arms she held a small whimpering bundle wrapped in a shawl.

"You have a son, Robert," she said quietly, turning the babe slightly so he could see better.

"*Mein Sohn*," he whispered, tenderly stroking the babe's still damp hair. "Thank you Ellen," and he leaned in to gently kiss her and then the babe.

"What will we call him?"

"I am thinking that Gustav would be a good name for him, after my younger brother, and Wilhelm – William, after my father, and maybe ... Albert – your father's middle name?"

And so now they were a little family of four and Willie, as he was always called, grew strong and thrived, and just over a month later he was baptised at the Parish Church in Killyleagh where Robert and Ellen had been married.

Reluctantly Robert had to admit that relying solely on getting work to crew the odd ship was not going to be enough for his family's future. One warm summer's day in July, he and Ellen were walking into Killyleagh to get some provisions and while they were there, to visit Ellen's parents and catch up on some local gossip.

As they walked, Robert took a deep breath and started to tentatively outline his thoughts about their future. If he used what he had managed to save over the last few years, and perhaps borrowed some if necessary, they could live in the house in Toye but adapt the adjoining building into a small general store. As it was, they had passed quite a few outlying cottages and small farms, and unless the occupants had transport into Shrigley or Killyleagh, they had a long journey there and back to get provisions. He would make some enquiries and also have a word with James, her brother, who was now baker in Killyleagh, and see what he thought of the idea.

The two men withdrew to the public bar for a pint of porter and Robert outlined his ideas to James. After some initial cautiousness, James agreed that there was merit in the scheme and that it would be a better bet than relying on the odd sailing job coming up.

Robert spent any available time over the next few days and weeks clearing out the adjoining outbuilding and putting in a counter and some shelves in preparation for starting to stock it out. He could not afford a huge outlay on goods, but decided to concentrate in the first place on items which would be heavy for people to carry from town. Borrowing a cart and horse for the day, he loaded up with sacks of flour (purchased from James), oats, and dried beans. Also other necessities like boxes of candles and barrels of lamp oil. Finally he added a few, less essential items like sugar, jam and apples. As a last minute addition, he took a few jars of toffees and boiled sweets. He had made a deal with some of the local merchants, like James, to buy at slightly above cost price but below their retail price, as a trial, and if successful, he would place regular orders in bulk and collect from them weekly.

On the way back from stocking the 'shop' in Toye, he detoured via the various smallholdings and cottages he passed on the way, winding the cart up bumpy farm tracks, to speak to the occupants and tell them that he would soon be open for business, and shortly would be able to take orders for any particular items they required, thus saving them a four mile walk to and from Killyleagh, loaded down with purchases or the need to arrange for a delivery from town.

And so began a new chapter in their lives. It was a bit of a gamble, but Robert was determined to make a go of it. And he was soon proved right.

CHAPTER FORTY-EIGHT

1879 onwards

Over the next year or so, Robert put all his efforts into the business in Toye. Soon he had a growing number of customers from the local area, as well as regular orders for deliveries. He decided to use some of the profits to buy a horse and cart, rather than hiring it when necessary, and Billy McGibbon, the blacksmith who lived opposite them, was useful to have on hand to replace a slipped horseshoe or mend a snapped bit.

Ellen fell pregnant again and in the March of 1880 gave birth to another son they named Robert Hugh. Robert's business was now becoming established and he was able to extend the goods he could supply, in line with the demands of his customers. As he could deliver goods to outlying hamlets, he was often covering a wider area than ever, and extending his customer base. He was soon a familiar sight coming up the road, with his buttoned-up mariner's jacket and still wearing his hat with the black shiny peak. Bit by bit he was able to repay the loans he had taken out, and using some of the profits, was able to add some creature comforts for the house. His biggest extravagance was a large rug for the main room and a rocking chair for Ellen in the kitchen. He also bought some little tin soldiers for the boys – something they would enjoy one day, he was sure.

It was drawing into the autumn of that year when the post boy came along one afternoon with a letter addressed to 'Herr Kannenberg'. It was addressed to them at their house in Breakey's Brae in Killyleagh, and it had obviously travelled far. It was with some trepidation that Robert opened the thick creamy paper and smoothed out the dust-smudged creases. It was from his brother August in Berlin, where he was now a successful businessman owning a large *apotheke* there.

Mein Lieber Bruder Robert..... *6th August 1880*

My dear brother Robert,

It saddens me to have to tell you that our sainted mother departed this life on 27th of July this year. As you know, she was living with our sister Marie, her husband Julius Kedesdy and their two young sons in Berlin. Marie was with our mother when she passed from this life to join her beloved husband and our beloved father, who was taken from us prematurely. May she rest in peace.

We do not know how you are doing in Ireland. We heard from the letter you wrote her a few years ago that you married and have a daughter.

You may write to me or our sister Marie – I have enclosed the addresses.

We hope you are well and that good fortune is with you.

With great sadness,
I remain,
Your brother, Auguste

Mit großer Trauer
Ich verbleibe,
Dein Bruder Auguste

Robert slumped down on the chair by the table in the kitchen, while Ellen looked on, alarmed by the obvious distress etched on his face. As he buried his face in his hands, the letter fell to the floor beneath his feet where Willie picked it up and attempted to put it in his mouth. Taking it from him, Ellen gave him a crust to chew on, and putting her arms around Robert, begged him to tell her what was wrong. Unable to read the German, she could not understand the cause of his obvious distress. Feeling his shoulders heaving under her hand, she could only rub his back and try to comfort him. Little Louise came in and froze when she saw her Dada looking so upset and immediately her face crumpled and her bottom lip quivered. Beckoning her over, Ellen encircled her with her other arm and together they tried to comfort Robert.

Later, Robert explained the content of the letter, and then realised that even though they were many miles apart, the tug felt by the bond of family transcends all.

Over the next few years Robert's business and his family expanded. Another son was born on the thirty-first of March 1882, whom they named Frederick Charles, then a daughter on the sixth of May 1883 whom they named Adelaide Matilda, and yet another son, Ernest Ludwig on the thirteenth of July 1884. So in the space of eight years, Ellen had borne him six children. The house rang with the sound of children's voices and Ellen was fully occupied looking after her little brood.

Robert was equally busy with the shop, which now was well established and frequented by the locals. Every week he would take the cart to Killyleagh, or even Strangford, and pick up goods from the quayside that he had ordered. He had a good reputation with the merchants and they gave him goods at a fair price, after he had haggled with them for the best deal. Sometimes he would take the cart into the sparsely populated countryside south west of Strangford, where he always found customers grateful for a regular visit. One of the places he liked to call in at was called Slievnagriddle, on his way to Saul, before heading back to Strangford, but he made everyone laugh because, no matter how he tried, he couldn't get his tongue round the pronunciation and always made Ellen giggle when he said he was off to 'Fiddlediddle'!

It was soon time to send Louise off to the local school at Tullymacknowes, where she learned her numbers and her ABCs from Miss Hutton. Soon she was followed by her brother Willie, who was never keen to go, and she had to drag him up Clay Road behind the house, to the little school on School Brae. Ellen was glad of the break for a few hours a day, leaving her with just the four little ones. And then she discovered she was pregnant again. It was a bitterly cold winter, and Ellen just felt she was never warm and was constantly tired. She went into labour on a cold sleety day in January when Robert was battling to reach a few of his outlying customers. By the time he came home, she had already given birth to the tiny babe which barely lived for a few minutes before it slipped away.

Robert was heartbroken when he came home, and realised that Ellen was under a tremendous strain. That winter she became very weak, and had a hacking cough for months. She tired easily and it was hard work to keep up with all the daily chores as well as looking after the little ones. Robert decided that they should employ a local woman to help her out and, through his brother-in-law James, he heard of a woman who had been a servant for someone in the town and was now seeking employment. She was an older woman, unmarried, but a reliable soul and a good worker. More than anything, Robert wanted someone else around the house when he was away, so it seemed the ideal move.

Ann Smith arrived one windswept late March morning and Ellen was immediately taken with her cheery demeanour and her rosy cheeks. Beneath her shawl, pulled tight around her head, there peeped a few strands of grey hair and beneath them her hazel green eyes twinkled. Initially Ellen felt rather strange asking her to do things around the house, but they soon settled into a routine and while Ann would tackle the washing or the cleaning, Ellen would be able to look after the little ones, often going into Killyleagh with Robert on the cart to the drapers to get cloth to make items of clothing for them, or to the bootmakers to supply new ones that had been outgrown. Even though they were regularly dressed in hand-me-downs for every-day wear, Ellen liked them to have some good clothes for Sundays and special days. The two boys, Willie and Robert, got into all sorts of trouble when she turned her back for just a minute. And three year old Adelaide would soon get dragged into their escapades, while baby Ernest was now toddling everywhere. Robert adapted part of one of the attached outbuildings as a room for Ann so that she could live in, and she soon became an indispensable part of their household.

Ellen began to get her colour back and eat better and Robert was relieved to see that she had some of her old energy back. On warm summer days, they would pack up the children onto the back of the cart, Ann as well, and go off to the coast for a picnic. By now Louise was a spindly ten year old, growing like a beanpole and good at keeping an eye on her younger siblings. Willie, as always, had to be different and loved to be awkward and do everything the opposite way, just to annoy his parents. Young Robert would be joining them both to go to school after the summer, and he was looking forward to striding up

School Brae and joining his friends at Miss Hutton's school at Tullymacknowes.

CHAPTER FORTY-NINE

1887 onwards

Robert's shop, which was technically a grocer's, but also stocked hardware and tools as well as sweets and stationery, was a great success and, supplemented by his delivery business, was doing a good trade. Often the children who lived in Shrigley would run up the road to Toye to play with the Kannenberg children and spend a farthing or a halfpenny on sweeties from the shop. These children were the families of the mill workers who worked at Martin's Flax Mill there. Rows of cottages had been built for the workers and there was now quite a population there. Around Toye there were also many farms, and the shop was the handiest place to come to buy what the famers could not grow or make for themselves.

On some evenings, a handful of men would drop by and Robert would sit with them on stools in the shop, exchanging talk of the success of the harvest, the weather, the price of barley, or whatever, and so it became a convivial meeting place, known for the hospitality of 'the German'. And more than talk, it seemed, was shared.

One night, as dusk had just departed and left the sky inky black and starless, two of the local constables kept watch on the shop at Toye from behind the hedge of the opposite field. Becoming cramped and cold, crouched in the dark, they soon wondered whether their mission was worth it, when a slash of light pierced the dark as a door opened and four men noisily made their farewells to their host, and set off, somewhat unsteadily, down the two roads in diverging directions.

A few nights later, the same two constables took watch and observed a similar scene played out. This time they had their orders to investigate, what appeared to be, flagrant flouting of the licensing rules as Kannenberg did not possess a licence to sell spirits or to serve it in his premises. They had been alerted by one or two of the local wives, whose husbands were returning late in the evening, rather the worse for wear, much to the annoyance of their spouses.

As the men headed off in their various directions, the constables leapt from their hiding place and ran over to the doorway of the shop, behind which Robert was in the process of closing up for the night.

"Open up!" came the order. "It's the Police!" And there followed some banging of fists upon the door to further illustrate the point.

The sound of the lock being turned presaged the reopening of the door, and as it swung back, Robert stood silhouetted in the lamplight from the room behind.

"Let us in! We have reason to believe that you are selling spirits illegally and without a licence, and what is more, you also have no licence to serve and charge for spirits on these premises. We have come to search the premises and detain you for further questioning, should we find that this is the case."

Looking bemused, Robert stood back and allowed them entry. By now, the noise had awoken Ellen, who was already in bed in the adjoining house. Wrapping her shawl around her nightgown, and holding a candle, she came across the yard and entered the shop from the rear entrance. What greeted her was the sight of the two constables looking behind boxes, into barrels and sacks, opening cupboards and pulling out drawers, not concealing their apparent frustration at not having found, thus far, what they had come looking for.

"What is happening Robert?" she asked, alarmed at the sight of the two uniformed men she recognised from the Constabulary on Back Street in the town.

"It's alright Ellen. They are mistaken. There is nothing to worry about. Go back to bed."

And with that, he took her by her shoulders and turned her about, propelling her towards the door.

"I will be in soon, once I have bid goodnight to these gentlemen and locked up the shop. Off you go."

After another fifteen minutes or so, having satisfied themselves that there was not a sign of a bottle, a barrel or a cask of any intoxicating liquor to be found, they bade him goodnight, but warned him that should they have reason to believe that he was indeed in breach of the law, they would return. At which Robert merely smiled and ensured them that he understood perfectly, but that they need not bother as he had nothing to hide.

Standing in the doorway, he watched as the two men made their way down the road in the direction of the town.

Returning to the shop, he straightened the items upon the shelves that had been disordered in the search, returned a heap of apples spilled from their crate and tidied away the stools to the side of the room. Finally he looked up to the ceiling from which hung thin ropes holding a variety of oil lamps for sale. Stretching up, he pulled on one of the ropes which were wound round pulleys, and lowered the lamp. The contents of the glass bowl shifted, as the pulley ratcheted down, and then came to rest in front of Robert. With a smile, he removed the glass chimney and the lamp wick assembly and dipped a small glass into the liquid, which he then sat on the wooden counter. Replacing the chimney and wick assembly, he pulled again on the rope, raising the lamp to join its companions, where they were suspended in the roof space above.

Turning to the glass on the counter, he took a sniff, smiled and threw the contents down his throat, then exhaled, muttering "*Das ist gut.*" What the constables didn't know, and what the men did, was that Robert had a lucrative little business going in brewing his own liquor and running a *shebeen* for his friends. He never discovered who had tipped them off, and the police never did find out why the local men seemed to enter the shop at Toye sober, and return, to their less than amused wives, the worse for wear.

The following July, Ellen produced another son whom they named Thomas Henry, or Harry, as he was always known. And less than a year after that, in her thirty-ninth year, she discovered she was yet again with child. As her pregnancy progressed, she felt that this one was different to all the others, and indeed she seemed to grow bigger more quickly, and seemed to be even more sapped of any energy. Thankfully she had Ann to take some of the load off her, as she now was certain from the feel of her belly that she was expecting twins. One cold day in December 1889 she went into labour and gave birth in the afternoon to two tiny baby boys. The first they named Oswald Victor and his younger brother, by ten minutes, they named August Theodore. Both were very small and weak, and neither seemed to thrive, but as the days went on it appeared that little Oswald was failing. He fed poorly and then often threw up what little he had taken. Just over two weeks into his little life, he quietly passed away in his crib next to his younger brother August.

That was to be Ellen's final pregnancy and now with eight surviving children, they were to build a secure future for them. Robert often mused over his own childhood, when he had been the second youngest of six children. What he had lacked was the firm hand of a father, having lost him when he was less than three years old. In fact, he truly could not recall any memories of his father, only remembering shadows of recollections from his older siblings or his mother. And now here he was, father of two girls and six boys. Different characters all. He secretly thought that Willie was most like him in character. His mother used a good Ulster-Scots word to describe him – '*thrawn*'. He was stubborn and never accepted advice. He would go his own way, never thinking about the consequences. Headstrong, wilful and quick to explode into a temper. But nevertheless, he was a staunch ally to his younger brothers when they got into scrapes at school with other boys – you always wanted Willie Kannenberg on your side. Robert was a quiet gentle lad with a strong sense of right and wrong. Fred was tall and lanky and never still. He even won third prize in a boy's race when he was ten, at an athletics meeting in Downpatrick. Adelaide was like her mother in so many ways. She was very attached to her Magilton grandparents and spent a lot of time with them. Ernest was another lanky lad and he was never happier than when helping in the shop, playing at being the shopkeeper. Robert would let him sort the shelves and weigh out the bags of sugar and, when none of the others was looking, Robert would pop a sweet into his little mouth and together they would share a secret wink. Harry was good with his hands, always making things out of bits and pieces, not particularly scholarly but adept at inventing little toys to keep his youngest brother, baby

Theo, amused. And of course Louise, the oldest of the children, now almost like a second mother to the youngest ones, taking them blackberry picking along the hedgerows or walking down to the coast to tire them out and use up all their pent-up energy.

And Ellen – she would often stand back a little when her family were gathered around the large table in the kitchen, and look at their faces and enjoy listening to the babble of their conversations. The quiet ones, the wild ones, the gentle ones – yet all of them a mix of her and Robert. They had heard some stories from him about the Prussian family far away and it saddened her to think that they would never meet. Thankfully none of the boys were keen to be sailors, but who knew where their lives might lead them. Their father had provided well for them – and her. They were comfortably off, not by any means wealthy but able to live within their means and have a bit left over for little treats and comforts. And that, she realised, was all that she really wanted from her life. It was all here, in this cosy kitchen full of life, laughter and love.

EPILOGUE

Toye, Co Down, N. Ireland 2001

It is a warm day in July and I am standing at a fork in the road, looking at the white painted gable of a two storey house. In my hand I hold a photograph of a painting of the house, done before the extra floor was added, and I can clearly see, high up on the gable, that the artist has added a painted board with TOYE written on it. On the angled wall, which is the front of the building, is the indication of another signboard with writing, and I wonder what it might have said. Lifting my eyes again to the scene in front of me, and watching out for cars which come swishing past at intervals along this busy road, I try to imprint the image on my mind. Then I focus my camera and take some shots to have it forever made permanent, enshrined in film.

Here is where the invisible string has pulled me to. Here is where I have come, to connect the two loose ends that have left me feeling unattached, with a sense of something not quite finished, not complete, a circle not fully joined up.

A year ago I stood on a bridge in Ueckermünde looking at the scene in front of me and trying to also imprint that one in my mind. From there spun out a string which was trying to tether me to my past. I flung it out like a lasso to encompass all the people and places and stories that I had never even known, but yet were so much part of me. And now I had found the other end and I was aiming to make that bond secure.

All the knowledge that I have discovered since that day

has totally blown me away with its intricacy and variety. Some of it felt so familiar, even though I had never heard it before. Some was astonishing, amazing and quite frankly, mind blowing. And some of it was very ordinary and mundane, but nevertheless, utterly compelling.

In my search I have travelled through four centuries of records, charting the lives of men, women and children, who were destined to give me just a shred of their DNA, never knowing where their line would reach.

And I am here, like a full stop at the end of a sentence. Like a line drawn under a total. I am the result of all their loving, and fighting, and crying, and laughing, and living, and dying.

I have learned so much about some of my antecedents, and not very much about others. I am now able to almost reach out and touch three of them, and I know that one day I am going to write their stories as best I can with the facts I have learned. I cannot know if they will be in any way faithful to their actual experiences, but I hope that they will display some measure of possibility.

I am the seven times great-granddaughter of Christian Kannenberg born in about 1620 in some far flung part of Europe.

I hope he would be proud to know me.

LIST OF CHARACTERS

Historical Characters

PART ONE

Johann Karl-Alexander Kannenberg – apothecary and innkeeper
Charlotte Schuler – Johann's wife
Karl Wilhelm Ludwig Kannenberg – Johann's son; doctor, obstetrician/ man-midwife and surgeon
Otto Albrecht Friedrich Kannenberg – Johann's brother; Supreme Court judge
Ernestina Groote – second wife of Otto
Johanna & Dorothea Kannenberg – sisters of Johann
Martin Friedrich Kannenberg – Johann's grandfather – gold, silver and silk buttonmaker
Justine Sollin – midwife

PART TWO

Tutors at the Friedrich Wilhelm Institute for Medicine and Surgery

Professor Rudolphus
Professor Knape
Dr Turte
Dr Hufeland
Dr Kluge
Dr Schlemm
Dr Rust
Dr de Gräfe
Dr Osann
Dr Dieffenbach
Dr Wolff
Dr Bartels
Dr Trustedt
Dr Jüngken

Karoline Sorge – wife of Dr Karl
(Gustav) Sorge – father of Karoline; police constable
Barbara Schallet – midwife
Dr Carl Heinrich Wahlstab – local doctor
Dr Ernst Friedrich Leonhardt – local doctor
Friedrich Alü – barber surgeon
Georg Schallehn – apothecary

Marie Charlotte Henriette Kannenberg – daughter of Dr Karl
Ernst Karl Theodore Kannenberg – son of Dr Karl

Karl August Kannenberg – son of Dr Karl
Henriette Louise Kannenberg – daughter of Dr Karl
Karl Robert Kannenberg – son of Dr Karl
Karl Gustav Kannenberg – son of Dr Karl

Therese Jess – wife of Ernst Kannenberg; children Ernst, Hans, Elizabeth and Gertrud
Mierke – husband of Henriette Kannenberg
Marie Hille – wife of Gustav Kannenberg
Julius Kedesdy – husband of Marie Kannenberg
Vilhauer – business partner of August Kannenberg

PART THREE
Joseph Gilmore – ship owner
Ellen Magilton – wife of Robert Kannenberg
Hugh Magilton – father of Ellen
Margaret Dick – mother of Ellen
James, Thomas, Hugh, Eliza, Mary, Frances and Adelaide Magilton – Ellen's siblings
John Dick – Margaret's brother
Reverend Moeran – minister in Killyleagh

Killyleagh shopkeepers
Cleland – draper
Guiney – postal officer
Furey – grocer
Madine – butcher
Girven – bootmaker
Mary Field – draper

Margaret Henriette Louise Kannenberg – daughter of Robert
Gustav William Albert (Willie) Kannenberg – son of Robert
Frederick Charles Kannenberg (Fred) Kannenberg – son of Robert
Adelaide Matilda Kannenberg – daughter of Robert

Ernest Ludwig Kannenberg – son of Robert
Thomas Henry Kannenberg (Harry) – son of Robert
Oswald Victor Kannenberg – twin son of Robert
August Theodore Kannenberg – twin son of Robert

Ann Smith – servant
Miss Hutton – schoolmistress at Tullymacknowes school

Imaginary Characters

PART ONE
Sophia – sister of Charlotte Schuler
Dr Barthelt – local doctor
Franz Grossen – husband of Sophia; shoemaker
Maximilian de Gräfe – brother of Dr de Gräfe
Friedrich Grossen – son of Sophia and Franz
Herr Volk – schoolmaster
Herr Bernd Wenzel – Direktor of Seddin school

PART TWO
Maria Sorge – mother of Karoline
Alexander Kannenberg – son of Otto
Emelie Kannenberg – daughter of Otto
Friedrich, Henriette, Ludwig, Dorothea and Christian Grossen – children of Franz and Sophia
Luise Schroeder – fianceé of Alexander Kannenberg
Emil Benke – manager of the Inn
Bruno Schultz – fiancé of Emelie
Agatha – widow; married Franz Grossen
Zeigler – town councillor
Herr Schoenberg – shipyard owner
Susann – servant to the Kannenbergs
Theo Schallehn – son of the apothecary

PART THREE
Gunther – shipmate on the '*Adler*'
Peggy – public house owner
Jimmy and Sarah Geddis - with whom Robert lodged
Mary Mulligan - public house owner
Patrick McArdle – crewman of the 'Friends'
Joseph - crewman of the 'Friends'
Willie - crewman of the 'Friends'
Billy McGibbon – blacksmith at Toye

ACKNOWLEDGEMENTS

I am indebted to Freeform Productions, whose research for the programme they made about my family in 2000 unwittingly set this project in motion. Without their German research I could not have begun this journey. I must also thank my friend Iris Mathers for advising me on the midwifery details and my friend Irene Clayton for reading the draft and offering encouragement, suggestions and comments. Thanks also to members of AGFHS who offered to help out with some German translations. Old images and information from members of the Old Pictures of Killyleagh and Shrigley Facebook page were of great help. Background information about the South Rock/Kilwarlin Light and Cloughey coastguard was gratefully received from Jim Brown. Heartful thanks to my friend Jim Rae, the talented maritime artist, who painted the image for the paperback book's cover. I am also indebted to Nathan Dylan Goodwin, author of historical genealogical crime mystery novels, who kindly offered his advice and support. Various online sites contributed to my understanding of the places and times in the book but I also found the following books of great help: *Iron Kingdom: the Rise and Downfall of Prussia 1600 - 1947* by Christopher Clark (Penguin 2007); *Health and Healing in Eighteenth-Century Germany by Mary Lindemann* (The John Hopkins Universtity Press 1996); *Becoming a Physician: Medical Education in Great Britain, France, German, and the United States 1750 - 1945* by Thomas Neville Bonnet (Oxford Universtity Press 1995).

And finally, of course, huge thanks must go to my partner Steve for putting up with late meals and listening to me reading excerpts to him over the dinner table.

ABOUT THE AUTHOR

Leona J Thomas

Leona retired after 40 years of teaching in Edinburgh, where she was born and grew up.

An amateur genealogist, she had a once-in-a-lifetime experience when a TV company chose her extraordinary ancestors to be the focus of a documentary. in 2000. What she learned from this inspired her to do further research of her own and from it came this book, which she put together during the coronovirus lockdown of 2020.

Leona lives with Steve, her partner of over thirty years, and an adorable cat called Daisy.

BOOKS BY THIS AUTHOR

Through Ice And Fire: A Russian Arctic Convoy Diary 1942

On the Russian Arctic convoys in 1942, Leonard H. Thomas kept a secret notebook from which he later wrote his memoirs. These contained many well-observed details of life onboard his ship, HMS Ulster Queen. He detailed observations of the hardships that followed when they endured being at action stations and locked in the engine room, under fire from the skies above and the sea below, and only able to guess at what was happening from the cacophony of sounds they could hear. Thomas tells of how the crew suffered from an appalling lack of food, the intense cold, and the stark conditions endured for weeks on end berthed in Archangel in the cold of the approaching Russian winter. There are also insights about the morale of the men and lighter moments when their humour kept them going.

These stories can now be told as his daughter has edited them into an account that illustrates the fortitude and bravery of the men who sailed through ice and fire to further the war effort so far from home.

Printed in Great Britain
by Amazon

45139746R00156